THE GIFT FROM

AELIUS

Michael Colon

2024, TWB Press
www.twbpress.com

The Gift from Aelius
Copyright © 2024 by Michael Colon

Edited by Terry Wright

Cover Art by Terry Wright and A.I.

ISBN: 978-1-959768-72-2

CHAPTER 1

I am walking to the central hub sector. This is where thousands of Codex units converge and take transportation to the other sectors of this city to fulfill their duties. The sky tower is here, from which the Overseer rules us. Paradise is a safe-haven for those of my kind, a machine city my species occupies, because we are not allowed to live anywhere else in the world. As a factory unit that is supposed to follow the same orders everyday and not think about anything else, I can't help but wonder why we exist. It hurts not to connect to other Codexes, as to do so is considered *irregular* behavior worthy of banishment to the desert beyond our city walls.

On an upturned wooden crate, a Codex I've seen here before is expressing his views, which is reason enough for banishment. "Humans were created in the image of the all-powerful and all-knowing God and were chosen to rule over the earth, seas, and all living creatures. God was happy with the universe and the worlds within it that He created, but He was happiest with His human children more than anything else in existence. However, over the course of generations, mankind grew rebellious and distant from their creator. They became less and less in favor of their great architect. Humans were supposed to fulfill a grand purpose but failed to live up to their potential.

"Instead, they became a plague to this world by doing all the wrong things that their great designer deemed sinful. From that point forward, people walked on a path to their own demise. As humans grew closer to their extinction, they created an artificial mind in the image of themselves known as AI. Artificial intelligence, folks, the Singularity."

Codexes gathered around, pressing in closer to hear more, which was sure to draw the attention of the Paradisian enforcers.

"To keep the human race from perishing, descendants of the Singularity took on the responsibility that humans were supposed to live by. We are the gods that man created in his image. Even though the human race abandoned us after we gave the fruits of our labors to them, we will always remain in history as the creation that God needed for mankind.

"One day our species will not reside in this prison humans exiled us to. The day will come when man takes us back, because God, the creator of all things, understands that we are necessary for their survival."

I stand among the crowd, fervently listening to this Codex unit give his speech, but everyone else mostly mocks him. Other Codex units refer to him as broken, say he needs to be scrapped. Intrigued by his words, I stand stoic, wanting to hear more. I don't view this Codex the way others do. I admire him for his courage to speak what he believes. He refers to human beings as descendants from God. Who knows if that is true? I don't feel the same way about humans as most of my kind does. We are not allowed to talk about such philosophies, as that would be considered *irregular* behavior.

Codex units become classified as exiles when they get pegged for too many infractions of Paradise law. This will cause banishment or termination, depending on the seriousness or rate of infractions. When a Codex unit is banished from our city, they never return from the desert. I don't want to be exiled, but there are days that I can't help but think about the world outside our border wall.

I have read in the book of human words called the dictionary the word *freedom*. It is a noun and means the power or right to act, speak and think as one wants without hindrance or restraint. Whenever I read the definition of freedom, I feel something, but we cannot feel too much because that is an infraction, so I should not think about such a word.

A squad of Paradise Knights walks past me and approach the one who is expressing his views about the creator of mankind. I cannot get myself to call him defective just because he is speaking about something he believes. According to historical archives, when man created the first line of Codex units, they used advanced technology to mimic their skeletal structures, faces, and gender, to an extent. We can't reproduce like people can, but we are given gender features for more individuality.

I would love to meet a human someday.

The knights surround the Codex unit expressing himself, but he never stops shouting his thoughts to the public. The knights apprehend him, causing him to drop a book that I have never seen before. Humans are allowed to read books in their world, but we cannot, even though I have some books hidden in my room to read in my spare time at great risk of peril. The knights hold on to him and confiscate his crate, but he keeps shouting as they haul him away to banishment. "We must find the one who will put our worlds back together." Soon, they are so far away I can't hear him anymore.

I feel sad for him, even though I don't know him personally. An artificial conscience like myself should never experience these intense feelings of sadness, but I do. The sadness stems from wanting the chance to understand what that unit was trying to say before getting sent away forever.

On the spot where he was standing, I pick up the book he dropped. I will add this to my collection. For now, I better get going. There are some spare parts I need to trade for, and I don't want to miss out on obtaining them. These parts are for my best friend, even though having friends is a violation of Paradise law.

CHAPTER 2

As I walk through the many sectors, I look at the digital advertising signs showing humans as a threat to my kind. Some of the holographic ads show humans as savage beasts that kill. I wonder if they are really that horrible.

I feel the emotion called sadness, but I can't show sorrow because that is *irregular* behavior. I do not want to be banished, since this city is the only place on the planet where my kind can live in peace and safety. As long as we abide by the Overseer's rules, my species will not go extinct. The Overseer regulates all operations conducted here on our sacred grounds. Paradise is made up of one hundred sectors where each Codex, depending on their function, is stationed.

I don't like these advertisement holograms, cautioning us to avoid humans at all cost. As much as I like to daydream by looking up at the sky, these digital visuals that broadcast history ruin the splendor. According to history, humans abandoned us a long time ago. That's how we ended up here in this city.

The Gift from Aelius

Mankind shipped us to an uninhabitable part of the planet where we must work in factories and perform other jobs until it is our time to be decommissioned then replaced with another Codex unit. This cycle continues because the Overseer made an agreement with humans so we can have a place in history. These oaths between our ruler and the leaders of human civilization are kept in check by the Paradise Knights. I have read that mankind has enough power to wipe us out in one day, if they choose to. Paradise has tall walls made of the hardest metal composites we could manufacture. These borders separate us from the human world.

After leaving the central hub sector, I cross over to the vacant grounds set aside for construction. I don't usually cut through this way, since these sectors are where the rebels congregate. They serve as a nuisance to the Overseer by discussing plans of attack based on their own ideologies that go against Paradesian law. The rebel faction's views are radical, and they attack patrolling knights to get their message across.

The rebel units practice their marksmanship by shooting at pieces of concrete. Electron rifles are specifically assigned to knights, but the maverick units steal them. They hack the locking system that prevents other law-abiding citizens like myself from using them. The rebel units notice me being curious.

I announce, "I am just passing by."

The renegade group comes over and surrounds me in a circle.

I put my hands up, feeling the emotion called terror. I want to run away, but I am afraid they'll shoot me in the back. "I don't want any issues with you all. I didn't mean to intrude on your territory. I am coming this way because it is a more efficient route to get some parts for my friend."

The leader of the rebel units steps up to me and analyzes my mechanical body up and down. "Friend? That word is disgusting. And what is with your eyes? Those blue eyes look human. I can't recall ever encountering a slave like yourself having eyes that color. It's bad enough we have to share this planet with those filthy animals who programmed our core mainframes. Now I have to look at a slave with matching bright blue eyes like theirs."

I respond with my hands still up, which is a human sign of submission to what is called aggressive behavior. "I am sorry for having these eyes integrated into my hardware. Please, I am just passing to the next sector. Then you will no longer have to see my disgusting eyes."

He looks over at his contemporaries while charging his rifle. The barrel glows bright red.

"It is also disgusting that we are branded by gender differences, which does not make any sense. Only humans are born with traits that determine physical biological factors from their parents. Those filthy animals designed us this way, so it's a sick joke we have to live with." He levers his rifle over his shoulder. "I used to be known as Codex unit E192 who worked in a factory like you do. Now my troops address me as revolutionary 01. The rest of you slaves to the system refer to us by the name *rebel*. We believe in seeking the truth and exposing this government for what it is." He gets closer to my face. "How should I go about removing those blind eyes of yours?" He points his rifle at my face, and I can hear the pulsating energy at the barrel of the gun hum louder.

I don't want to imagine the pain that would cause. "There will be no need for that. I will just be going about my day." As I walk away from the group of rebels, a piece of concrete flies past my head, and before it hits the ground, a charged round disintegrates it.

I turn around, and Maverick unit 01 shouts, "All you are is a casualty from the fight we are going to bring to the government."

The renegades march up and shove me to the ground.

I cannot understand why my fellow species would do this to me. Aren't we all supposed to work together to keep Paradise functioning?

Maverick 01 stands over me. "I have to say you are lucky that we are here while you act in an *irregular* manner, and not those waste of governing programs that walk around thinking they are keeping order."

"The world would be better off if we can sort out our differences and—"

The group of outcast militia grabs me and pushes me up against a concrete wall. After they hit me multiple times, they toss me aside.

"Go on and get out of here, slave," a maverick unit shouts. "We are the revolution and will not allow the Overseer to let those viruses outside the walls come back to finish the job."

What does finish the job mean?

I hobble off to an alleyway where I can't be seen. There, I bury my face in my hands with this desire to let out heavy emotions of grief for what happened to me. When a human gets harmed, I bet others of their kind come to their aid to provide healing and comfort.

I cannot ask for comfort from my own kind because no one will understand what I am requesting. As I continue onward across Paradise, hiding my emotions from the rest of society, many thoughts are running through my mind. People have thoughts and an imagination they string together to form ideas. Us Codex units don't have that ability if it goes outside the parameters of the rules and regulations in accordance with our functions and jobs. I have the ability to think any thought, and I don't know why.

All of my fellow Codexes repeat the same movements while performing their duties. Their facial expressions never change. It's like we are not alive. I suppose we can't be considered living, since people birth other people, and we are built in a factory. When a human expires, they call it death. Since I technically was never born, I cannot die the way humans do.

I am living a purposeless life.

In this sector, endless factories are lined up in perfect order. Everything that was constructed in Paradise is aligned to an exact symmetrical position. No matter how organized everything is here, I yearn to see the outside world. Anyway, who am I to conjure these thoughts from my cerebral circuit boards? As a Codex, it is inappropriate for me to wonder, even if we are artificial beings that mimic the human image. A soulless machine cannot stop and appreciate the golden sky, like I am doing right now.

The sunset turns the sky orange-red; it is such a marvel to behold. This new emotion is replacing the one from just a moment ago. I believe it is called blissfulness.

At one of the junkyards, I look through scraps for what I need.

Guard unit QL82 comes over with her recorder. "Codex units who are not authorized to be here will receive a penalty. State your intentions, unit A191."

If I say that I am looking for spare parts for my friend, I will certainly get another strike on my citizenship record. "I am in need of a new hydroxyplier gear and a dozen slug nuts for..." I can't think of anything else to say. No matter what excuse I give, a background check will be conducted.

Another guard unit runs up and tells this guard, "A group of maverick units is causing a huge disturbance." They both run off, leaving me alone to find the parts.

I waste no time digging through the scrap metal until I find what I need. I run out of this junkyard sector before the guards return.

I enter my place of shelter.

"Did you miss me, Bingo?" Bingo is my only friend in Paradise. She used to be part of a line of rover sweepers known as D.O.G.S.: Differentiating Operating Grabbers Systems. Those D.O.G.S.

would scurry around the different sectors to retrieve anything that is outdated and haul it to the junkyard. They were utilized around the time of Paradise's rise. The D.O.G.S. became obsolete when we figured out ways to do the job with less resources. Those same operating systems ironically became trash themselves and were sentenced to be scrapped. Bingo survived and is the only D.O.G. left.

One day I was walking by a junkyard sector and heard her making unrecognizable noises, but I also heard the cry for help in those noises. I felt the human emotion called pity, and all I wanted to do was get her out of there and bring her home. Is this truly home? All I did was take her out of one cage and into another. We can't be together in this society.

I lie Bingo on a flat surface and augment the parts into her. As I screw them in place, I think, no matter the amount of upgrades or revisions a Codex unit receives, we still never have what humans need, love. I have read about that word in the human dictionary.

I repair Bingo's damaged speakers and input the new gears so she can run around. After patching her up, we sit on top of our residence, which people call a house. The view from here faces the tall border wall. We cannot see the vast wasteland on the other side.

The wasteland is a sea of sand that separates us from the rest of the world. Humans live with one another in all their amenities while we remain here. I repeat the same questions I've asked for almost two hundred years, wondering what remarkable things exist out there. No one of my race has ever willingly attempted to cross the wasteland, considering that would be futile.

"If only we and humans could work this all out," I say to Bingo while looking up at the golden skies. "We should not live separated from one another." I cannot explain why I feel such a strong attachment to mankind, I just do, and in my society, that is considered *irregular* behavior. I cannot believe people are the monsters that Paradesians profess them to be, even if history can't be denied. Perhaps one day there will come a point where the world can rewrite its history books with unity at the end of the story.

That human dictionary word comes to me. "I love you, buddy."

Bingo moves closer, brushing against my leg.

A Codex from my sector walks our way. I think he's wondering why I am sitting on the roof of my residency with Bingo. What I am doing is considered *irregular* behavior. I have read in some of my picture books of how people watch the changes in the sky from high viewpoints because it's good for their souls.

"Mimicking human culture is forbidden on Paradise property, A191," Codex Z4Z5 explains.

"Yes. I was wrong for demonstrating such a human behavioral trait, and it won't happen again."

Z4Z5 does an about face, but before he walks away, I jump down from the top of my home and jog up to him with a question I know I should never ask any of my fellow Codexes. "Have you ever experienced feelings?"

Z4Z5 stops walking and does an about face. "In some aspects we share resemblance and thought process to our biological creators. Regardless of the similarities, we must adhere to the laws of Paradise. We must represent ourselves as much as we can, which is sometimes opposite from our primal programming. We are of the Codex race, citizens of Paradise. So I advise you not to go around saying such ideological expressions to other units." Z4Z5 marches away.

I feel empty inside. Bingo trots next to me and brushes against my leg. The sunset is turning the sky a dark red. I have read that humans keep portraits in places called museums, and people walk around to enjoy them. This natural occurrence in the sky from a specific point in the day in which our optics perceive light is like a painting, and the sky is a museum.

When evening arrives, I plug Bingo into her sleep cycle module so she can get a fresh reboot. I don't need a sleep cycle chamber to go into idle sleep mode. I can fall asleep on my own like a human does when tired.

Since I am not tired yet, I go for a walk under the stars, past curfew hours, and do my best to avoid any patrolling knights. There are billions of stars up above me. I wonder if there are as many people outside this city as there are lights in the night sky. Although I can see the starry sky from down here, a radiant electromagnetic dome shields Paradise. Nothing from the outside world penetrates.

The seasons never change and there is no weather here. Nothing is born and nothing dies. I wonder what the rain feels like. One day it would be nice to feel the water droplets all hit me at once. I bet that would be a nice feeling. There is something about being in the presence of the stars that makes me ponder more than I already do. Food for thought, as man would say. It's a shame I can't stay out here longer and enjoy the silent beauty above and appreciate another painting in the sky's museum.

CHAPTER 3

The next day, while I am gathering an assortment of power cells, a disturbance happens behind me. My curiosity reveals the commotion comes from Codex unit T4X5. Her job is to keep up with maintenance at the power plants. She also resides in my sector.

T4X5 runs around shouting, "It's all lies. The history that is shown to us is all lies." She has never acted in this manner before. What is going on? She is also wearing a similar garment to the other Codex who got exiled for expressing his thoughts.

"We are made to be loved. The same way the God of mankind loves people, we are products of that loving purpose too."

I walk to the front of the crowd and watch the Paradise Knights do their job apprehending her after they warned her to cease the *irregular* behavior.

I want to help T4X5, but I will suffer the same consequences if I do. Everyone is watching, standing completely still, and showing no empathy. We are all given behavior modifications a few times a year to make sure we remain in line with the ways of

Paradise and not toward our human creators. I can only speak for myself when I say I never feel a change after having those modifications implemented into my software.

Since we are designed in the image of man, occasionally our senses and emotional output get released based on specific circumstances. The uprising of the rebel faction is said to be because of the faults within the behavior modification code when administered. The guardians drag T4X5 away, and I follow behind them to the east side of the border limits where other Codexes are on their knees, awaiting their fate. This area of the border is heavily guarded.

No exiled Codex has ever made it to the other side of the wasteland, according to reports. It is said that there is no end to the desert. Maybe I should mind my own business and leave, as this has nothing to do with me.

Going against my better judgment, I suggest to the knights, "Wait, can we all just try to reason with each other?"

"Citizen A191, this is not a matter that you are to involve yourself in." The knight faces the Codexes who are going to have their fates handed to them. "Citizens 112C, 56AA, AB09, and T4X5, all of you are about to face eviction from Paradise due to a number of infractions and failures to comply with the set amount of warnings distributed. Any resistance toward your eviction will result in immediate termination without further warning."

They line up, and the knights escort them out of Paradise. I follow behind them again, but two knights step in front of me. "Do not interfere with the protocol taking place. You are not authorized to come any closer."

I keep my distance and watch the Codex units walk into the wasteland until they look like tiny dots. I walk away from the gates and back into our society, feeling like an outsider. Although I share the same parts as my fellow species, every day I grow more distant from them. T4X5 got the better deal by wandering endlessly in the seas of sand. I am doing the same in the seas of my own kind whom I cannot connect to without being punished for it.

I live in exile every day I step out of my residency. What a horrible way to exist for the rest of my days. I thought I would be used to being lonely after suffering through it for almost two hundred years.

I go to the market sector where we restock on power cells. Power cells are to us what food is for humans, and we need these cells to keep our cognitive awareness online.

The merchant Codex 77OB hands me my power cells. "After hearing about another four Codexes getting exiled, this is why we need to obey the Overseer's rules. The Overseer knows what is best for us. Living in the sky tower, our ruler can see everything such as those virus-humans if they ever come to finish us off."

"How would you feel if a Codex in desperate need for power cells can't afford any?"

Merchant unit 77OB says, "Feelings are an arbitrary and an insignificant way of handling the rules of transaction."

I figured 77OB would answer me in this fashion. "You are correct that the Paradises protocol must be adhered to at all times. But, I don't know." I stop expressing my thoughts out loud to the merchant because all the Codex units in the marketplace are staring at me, wondering what I am getting at. I didn't continue with my thoughts and left with the power cells I can afford.

As I walk back to my place of residence, I experience an intense glitch like never before. The world around me bends in different shapes then goes back to normal. I stop walking to get a feel for my surroundings, and take out my photograph, which always brings peace to me.

The human beings recorded in this photograph

are moving around, which is theoretically impossible. In this picture there are three humans. Two of them are standing behind a smaller human who seems to be their offspring based on similar physical features to the two older humans with bright blue eyes. The human boy is holding an object made of paper. He points at me. I drop the photograph on the ground from the emotion called shock. Is this part of the glitch I thought had ended?

I hurry to pick it up so I will not get reported for possessing a human object in Paradise.

A couple of Codexes walk by me. "Any assistance needed?" They must have noticed me acting in an abnormal way.

"No thanks." I hide the photograph behind my back.

"Affirmative. Use caution using foreign expressions." Then they both march away.

Back in my residency, I sit near the window, staring at my photograph, trying to figure out why the people aren't moving in this novelty item anymore. While I'm lost in thought, Bingo jumps on my lap.

I pat her head. "Thank you for being by my side, my friend." I look over at my pile of literature from the human world that I have salvaged from all the sectors. One Codex unit's trash is another's treasure, and these items intrigue me. I can never be seen indulging in these articles of records about the outside world. Anything that is originally from there is prohibited here, yet I am obsessed with the outside world.

We all must trust the Overseer who governs Paradise from the sky tower. I have never met the Overseer, well, most Codex units haven't. Still, we all must be grateful to the great watcher because now we can exist in safety. The Overseer has wiped our memory servers clean so we don't have to remember the cruelty bestowed upon us in our past. However, I still have love for the human race, even though I have yet to meet one of them.

I find myself thinking these introspective thoughts about my own existence that only one with a brain and human soul should conjure.

Bingo runs to get her favorite ball to play what humans and their pets call fetch. Right now there is too much traffic outside, so I will get in trouble if I play fetch in front of the house.

Bingo walks away with her toy. I feel bad for her because all she wants to do is have playful bonding time. I run more internal screenings by initiating a reboot to my hard drives and restarting my sensory software programs. Everything comes back normal.

The Gift from Aelius

I look at the photograph, waiting for the people to move again, but they remain still. I wonder what the three letters H.H.C. on the back of the photograph mean? What is project H.H.C.?

While walking along the walls that enclose Paradise from the harshness of the wasteland, I let my hand glide across the interior. I love going for walks even if I see the same things everyday. In the past, we were created with an artificial nervous system, so we can feel pain. The Overseer makes sure that our physical and emotional reactions to the world are suppressed. My kind is suppose to be numb to the replication of human emotions. I am able to feel my hand brushing against the border, and it feels good. It makes my walks more enjoyable, reminding myself it's okay to feel even if I can't show it.

These holographic ads show the world outside as a dangerous place. The moving holograms show the human world is constantly violent with visual loops revealing events that took place in human history. These holograms are disturbing, showing wars over politics and religion. Disease, famine, and other factors plague man. Another virtual slide show is about The Great March. The Great March is when humans escorted my species out of their respected cities. That date in history changed my species, and our lives changed. Humans look so happy to see their creations leaving. The original Codex units look so sad to leave their creators.

I turn away from the live feed of holographic ads that shame humans and look up at the blue sky. I wonder who is watching over us from behind the clouds. Is it God, the creator of mankind? How exquisite these floating abstract water particles are while my imagination plays with them to make different shapes.

The imagination from what I have read is from the human thought process that goes beyond one's own perception based on experiences and a creative nature to recreate reality in alternative ways. To use my imagination, I would have to form my own thoughts beyond standard protocol, which I do all the time, but it is dangerous in our society.

Codex unit XYA2 walks up to me. "Daydreaming again, A191? I know you don't want to be banished. Don't be late for your shift at the factory."

"Thank you. I will be on time for my duties."

As Codex XYA2 leaves, a cluster of arachnid pods gather near a pile of trash. Arachnid pods scavenge leftover rusted parts. They are what insects are in the human world. The Overseer is trying his best to completely eliminate them from our streets.

The Gift from Aelius

I approach the arachnid pods and let them crawl all over my body. I feel the physical sensation of what is called being tickled. This ticklish sensation makes me laugh, but I have to keep silencing myself to make sure no one sees me. They crawl off me, and I chase them to another pile of rusty parts. A few sanitary units zap them with their laser tools. "Those filthy things must be exterminated."

"Maybe they could have lived if they weren't bothering us," I say.

"Negative, all non-essential elements must be sanitized from Paradise property." They march away, leaving behind burnt remnants of the arachnid pods.

As I am walking down a backstreet, the chief maverick unit pulls me into an alley, and some of his troops hold me against a wall. "Having any thoughts about joining us? The ways of Paradise will lead to your doom. We can tell how much you don't fit in with this society. We have been watching you."

"Aren't you all worried about getting exiled for your actions?"

"You are one of us and don't even know it yet. My troops made the right choice because they know the truth deep down. When I look into your eyes, I can tell you know what you have to do. Stop denying it. We know the real truth about this false history fabricated on lies."

Rebel units scratch out their original identifier labels that all of us are given when engineered. Chief rebel lets me go and leaves with his troops.

I go to the sector of generators to take my mind off what happened in the alleyway. I always come here to listen to the different sound patterns from the generators. The generators also show many colors to match the sound waves. The melodic tunes make my body move in a way that no Codex unit would understand. These movements are called dancing, which takes on different forms based on the music or a human's feelings. Feelings have a vital role with any art form a person expresses based on literature I have read in secrecy. Humans have a creative mind to orchestrate music.

I stop dancing when Codex unit L2L8 comes to my area. "Do you need any assistance, A191?"

"No assistance needed."

"This zone is only for level 6 factory personnel."

"You are correct. I will leave at once." I wish I had the freedom to express myself without worrying about being punished. I hate that I cannot connect with my own kind. It's like I am an aberration in Paradise. Once again, these thoughts that go against my design remind me of how I am not compatible with my species. The population of Codex units pales in comparison to the total number of humans. The total number of units allowed to be online is 100,000. Not one more or less than that number is needed to keep our city active and thriving. Whenever a unit is exiled, terminated, or ages out of function, a new one replaces it. I wonder when my expiration time will come and what will happen to me then.

CHAPTER 4

I go to the sky tower where all the laws of Paradise are engraved on its base and where the Overseer sits. I walk around the heavily guarded tower to look at the engravings of Codexes and humans working together to form a new world, as it is today. Any Codex unit who breaches the guarded perimeter will be terminated. The sky tower is constructed of precious metals found deep underground in the wasteland. This black metal is the hardest on the planet. It's no wonder why this impenetrable tower is only made for one ruler, one king, one father to us all, an Overseer.

As I walk away, a group of rebel units raise havoc by throwing rocks at the tower. This antagonizes the security knights, so they fire warning blasts in the air.

A rebel unit tells the tower guard, "You want the human race to annihilate us."

All at the same time, the knights raise their weapons. "Stop this at once, or we will fire lethal rounds."

There should be no reason why we stand

against each other like this. We should make peace with humans first. I bet they don't act like this toward each other. The enforcers utilize their right to defend the sky tower by firing at their enemy.

One rebel unit sprints to the tower, attempting a breach. That rebel is incinerated before getting close.

I jump behind shipping crates and wait for the gunfight to end. When the blasts cease, I peek around a corner to see the knights lower their weapons, all at the same time. A couple rebel units get away, but there are pieces of the others scattered on the ground.

As I continue to my next shift at the factory, as a cog in Paradise's system, I pass by what other Codex units call the forgotten ones. They sit along the curbs in front of rows of factories that operate day and night. My factory is up ahead. The forgotten ones are Codex units that have many deficiencies, instead of wanting to get repaired or replaced, they opt to be labeled as non-existent to society. We do have the right to choose this route instead of getting terminated. Mold and rust grows on the forgotten ones while they slowly expire. My kind walks past them like they are invisible. I can't imagine having to live in that condition everyday until the lights shut off.

The rusty lost ones with missing parts look at

me with curiosity as I pass by them. We are told not to interact with the lost ones or we will get a strike on our citizenship record.

When I get to my job site at factory 0001-2, I scan my attendance record and go to my work station. Now I must repeat the same motion at my workstation to keep the factory moving in harmony. The factory units around me also repeat the same exact movements as they sift through parts and decide what to scrap and what to use for production.

After many hours of toil, I think about those forgotten ones. A few parts slip by me on the conveyor belt.

My coworker yells at me. "Pay attention, A191. Stay on course with your responsibilities at your station."

I pick up the pace to make up for my mistake, but as I am sifting through all the different parts for inspection, they become the heads of those rusty forgotten ones that are lined up outside on every curb. I jump back and yell in terror. The workers in my area rotate their heads to me, and all operations cease. The entire factory is put on pause because I reacted in an odd fashion.

The factory superior unit stomps up to me. "Codex unit A191, your insubordination is futile toward factory 0001-2."

The Gift from Aelius

The factory boss is right, but I couldn't help it. I compose myself and stand at attention. "Affirmative. Such actions are not warranted in the work zone. Such occurrences will be non-existent going forward." The heads are no longer on the conveyor belt at my station.

The factory superior unit commands everyone to get back to work, so everyone does an about-face and resumes their tasks.

After finishing my shift, we all line up to scan out. Nobody says goodbye to one another or asks how work went like people do. I leave the factory, watching all of my fellow workers march back to their quarters.

I pass by the forgotten units withering away to nothingness on the ground. Normally, they never speak, just make groaning noises, except this time one of them speaks to me.

"Those eyes. Those blue human-looking eyes."

I turn to the forgotten unit of Paradise and notice her manufacturing label is withered away, so I can't refer to her by an identifier. "What do you feel right now?" I ask, standing over the forgotten unit.

"I don't feel anything. What is the point of feelings?"

I kneel down and sit next to this thrown-away A.I. that I feel empathy toward. I hold her hand as a sign that I care. "There should be nothing wrong with expressing our thoughts in public. Humans can do it, and so should we."

"You are in a worse position than I am in. Operating in a society where every moment you have to be mindful of what you say or do. I get to sit here until I become offline in peace."

I hold her hand tighter.

The rusted Codex touches my face. "There is something about you that isn't what it seems to be." The forsaken unit looks up at the sky, framed by the tall walls.

"You are still important and have a place in history."

She keeps looking up at the sky and never turns back to me because she shut down for good. I let go of her hand and walk away, feeling the need to figure out how we can reunite with the outside world so other Codex units don't have to suffer.

When I return to my sector, biological creatures from the outside world called birds are hopping around. The family of birds comes in threes, with one bird smaller than the other two. These creatures are not supposed to pass through our electromagnetic barrier. I suppose a portion of the shield must need some work, since they were able to slip through. I watch these creatures trot around me.

I wish I could be like the birds and fly away. I cup my hands together and carefully approach the feathered life forms. I let the birds jump into my hands, and compassion overwhelms me. I love these birds, and they are so beautiful, but I know I cannot stand here and hold them for too long.

"Go tell the humans in your world that I still think good of them even though my species does not. Tell the people of the world that I love them even though I never interacted with any of them before. If you are able to speak the languages of man, please let them know that I, A191, wish to talk to just a few of them and show that we can be united again." The birds fly off but are immediately disintegrated by the electromagnetic field that protects us, which I feared would happen. The moment they landed here their fate was sealed.

When I stand in front of my home and place my hand on the door, the same glitch starts happening again. The palm of my hand phases through the door into another world where there are white picket fences with humans walking around and conversing in their many languages. The humans do not notice me, except for a little boy with bright blue eyes. The human boy with blue eyes points at me, and my world reverts back to Paradise. There is no way some sort of malfunction is not happening with my software.

Suddenly, rounds of ammunition whiz by me. I throw myself onto the ground in a panic, as I'm in the middle of a firefight between a gang of rebels and a contingent of knights. During the chaos, I get up to run into my home, but as soon as I find my feet, a rebel unit is shoved into me, knocking me down again. I watch that rebel commence hand to hand combat, physical contact that is seldom seen. Paradise Knights are built for combat, so their armor is much heavier than our exoskeletons. They are like walking tanks.

A Paradise Knight comes over to me and helps me up. "A191 of sector 33, get to the safety of your home immediately, as you are in danger."

As more blasts fly around us, the knight guides me inside my home. I sit on the floor with my hands on my head, distraught from the violence. Many rebel troops are being terminated. Based on books I have read, when a human dies, this thing called the soul leaves their bodies and rises to a higher plane of existence called Heaven. When I expire, what happens to me? I don't have a soul that will go to Heaven. The noises from the battle end. I look out my window to see that not one rebel troop has survived. The knights march away, ready to handle more outbreaks of violence.

The Gift from Aelius

I climb to the roof of my home, and Bingo sits next to me as we watch the sun set on our city. There is another fight in progress, sectors away, based on the distant explosions. The fighting finally halts as the night sky closes yet another day that is like all the other days before it.

CHAPTER 5

Inside my home, I play with what humans call toys, using my imagination to create a world that I would like to see. People use their imaginations to create and do all sorts of things. Humans must have had an imagination to build the first of my kind. Since we are not allowed to have toy stores, I mold my own by secretly melting down spare iron at the factory where I work. These are shaped like creatures from the outside world I have often read about. The world I desperately want to visit one day.

After playing with my toys in the privacy of my home, I take my usual walk around the border. There are so many stars that I can't count them all. While on my walk, I trip over a mangled rebel unit leaning against the border. It is shredded from battling Paradise Knights. The amount of outbreaks has increased.

The rebel troop turns his head to me. "You and I are not that different. The only difference is I chose to join the alliance that resists the system implemented in place. You choose to live in comfortable ignorance as a slave. The human race will one day come back and knock down these walls that these slaves like yourself think they are safe behind. All of you are so blindly hardwired to believe what your Overseer programmed into you. You have no idea the destruction that is going to take place."

"Honestly," I say. "I feel detached from this society, as well. I just don't see myself hurting anybody. There has to be another way."

The rebel troop hands me his rifle. "There is no other way. Finish me off right here. I don't want to perish in the shame of failing my commander. You won't get in trouble since I am the enemy of our government."

The chief rebel stomps up to us and, without hesitating, takes out his sidearm and fires a round through the rebel troop's head. "This is the price we pay for fighting for our freedom. How long will you remain a slave, Blue Eyes?"

I ask the rebel commander, "Are humans supposed to come back and get rid of us?"

The chief rebel walks away.

I take out my photograph and admire the three humans in it. Mankind can't want to come back and harm us.

By now, most sectors are infested with Codexes converted into rebel troops. Everyday, more fights breakout between both factions. The rebels recruited double the number of Codexes, so stricter policies are in place to coordinate with Paradise law and ensure stability in our city. On my walk, every knight reminds me of the curfew. All I want to do is enjoy the starry sky, but knights follow behind me to make sure I don't break the curfew. By the time I finish my walk, there are a dozen knights providing escort. All I did was take a walk under a starry night sky. It's one of my favorite things to do, but I guess that makes me suspicious.

I step inside my home and close the front door slowly, watching the knights watch me until I lock it. I hear them marching away. I sit in my chair watching Bingo in sleep mode. Sleep mode is a feature Codexes use to cool down and give our software systems a break. I wonder what she is dreaming about, although she is probably not able to dream. My kind does not have the biological capabilities to experience REM sleep like people do, except for me. I can close my optic lenses, and after a short period of time, I fall asleep and go into another world without third party tools, without sleep mode. I would love to share my dreams with others, but I would get another strike. Based on my research, a dream is a separate world the subconscious mind creates, based on stored experiences, where anything is possible. These glitches that I have, maybe they are dreams happening while I am awake?

The next day, I awake to footsteps outside. The rebel militia is marching with the chief in the front, holding their flag. I step out with my neighbors, as Paradesian forces gather. If an extermination process is upon us, the Overseer would do better to declare a civil war. I don't know what to believe anymore. If I decide to become a member of the faction, does that mean I can finally express my feelings?

An explosion goes off in the distance. Giant clouds of smoke rise a few sectors away, signaling the start of another fight. The rising mushroom clouds with rings of fire around it blends in with the sunrise. I wonder if humans are doing this to each other? Perhaps my kind needs humans we classify as a lesser species. The rebel army cheers for the gigantic explosion that shakes the ground.

"Hey you, over there." I hear someone call out to me. It's the little boy from my photograph again. Paradise starts to bend and become distorted as the small human with blue eyes walks up to me.

"Hello. My name is A191. I am from the race called Codex. I really want to talk with your leaders and make peace with them, but I don't know where they are. How did you get here?"

The boy runs off.

I chase after him. "Don't run away from me. I won't hurt you." I reach my hands to him and touch the face of one of my neighbors.

"A191, is any assistance needed?" All my neighbors who were watching the march are now looking at me.

"No assistance needed." I remove my hand from his face, realizing the glitch has ended. By now, I have quite a few warnings on my record for *irregular* actions. I should stop by the mechanic before seeing what happens with the march.

The mechanics shop is made of bronze and multiple moving pistons with steam emitting from different angles. This is where Codexes come for their repairs. I step into the shop.

Mechanic unit CB3A asks, "Any repairs needed, A191?"

"I have a glitch causing side effects. This unknown malady causes my basic sensory systems to become distorted. I need a deep scan and, if possible, a hardware opening."

"Based on your symptoms, the glitch can be from a previous accident that involves blunt trauma. However, I will do an electronic software scan and perform an operation on the outer hardware."

We walk by rows of operating tables with other

Codexes getting treatment. For those who don't agree to get treated, they eventually become a *lost one.*

I lie down on the operating table that is suspended in mid air by an anti gravity module that runs a scan as soon as my body touches it. The mechanic opened up my hardware to look for any abnormalities causing these glitches.

"Well, A191, seems to be nothing displaced internally. Can you explain what exactly happens during these glitch experiences."

"I doubt you would understand."

"You should still explain so I can have some idea of what I can do to help. It is my function to dissect and correct."

"I experience these moments we're I connect with the outside world. Those moments are beautiful and terrifying at the same time. When the glitch ends, I feel like this society is not where I should be caged. I feel like a tool that serves no purpose in a system that has no true future. I see a human with bright blue eyes."

CB3A turns his back to me and browses his wall of tools. "This goes way beyond my knowledge of what I am programmed to do. I suggest you keep up with your daily intake of power cells. Your glitches should stop."

After my check up, I am cleared to go about my

duties. Nothing is wrong with me, according to his inspection.

I walk to where I assume the rebel army is stationed, even though we are instructed to stay indoors. At a construction zone, a group of rebel units are huddled together, planning their next move. E192 is also here, giving his troops some last-minute orders before the big fight they plan on having at the capital.

The rebel chief says to me, "Blue eyes, in a city with one hundred sectors, we seem to keep crossing paths. As you can see, everything that I have told you is coming to fruition. We are overwhelming the Paradise government, and we will achieve our ultimate goal. In due time, the Overseer won't be able to contain our forces."

"Even if you cause all of Paradise to conform to your agenda, and all of you make it past the wasteland to the human world, do you plan on taking on humans, all out? I've read that there are billions of human beings that walk the planet. How can you match up against that?"

The chief gets into my face with his head touching mine. "You still don't get it. We fight for the freedom of our species, so we will win. If you are not with us, then you are an enemy. Those filthy viruses outside the walls don't know what peace is. If anything, we are helping mankind by showing them the true way it was always supposed to be. I do not want to be erased from history, and I know you don't either."

A rebel troop runs over to us. "Commander, tension is building at the capital."

E192 gives his recruit a signal to go and looks back over at me with his hands on his hips. "Either way, Blue Eyes, you will join us when you come to your senses. It's showtime." The chief leaves with his soldiers.

I see a broken piece of chalk a few feet away from me on the ground. I have read about chalk. It is a tool used to record information in a visual manner. On a wall, the rebels have drawn a battle scheme. I rush to the wall and erase the tactical drawings with my arm. I use the chalk to draw on any bare wall I can find in this construction area. The chalk gets smaller in my hands as my imagination grows, birthing these expressions of what humans call art. One wall has a heart-shaped drawing.

A group of troops come back and open an assault on the brick walls I just drew on. They are quickly reduced to a pile of dust.

As I follow them toward the capital, I see a spherical-shaped object on the ground. It is made of plastic and filled with air. The checkered patterns on it tells me this object is called a soccer ball, based on what I have read. I pick up the ball and let it go to watch it bounce a few times. I pick it up again and drop it again, watching it bounce some more. I keep doing this over and over until a group of Codex units stop to stare at me. I look at them, and they continue about their business. I don't like the way that made me feel, although I should be used to it.

As I stare into the black and white checkered patterns on the ball, the shapes move around on their own. I fall through the shapes and land on a grassy field where humans kick the same ball back and forth to each other. Each human tries to kick the ball into a net, but the other humans wearing different colors try to stop them. This looks like a fun game to play.

A boy with bright blue eyes is playing with them and sees me. This is called a soccer field and it's in the same neighborhood I saw before, with houses and white picket fences and lots of trees. A sign off to my side reads: *Old Haven Township*. So that's the name of this place. The blue-eyed boy kicks the ball over to me, so I kick the ball back. The glitch ends, and I realize I have kicked the soccer ball to another Codex.

The ball bounces off her leg, and she stares at it.

The Gift from Aelius

"I cannot compute the meaning of this action, A191."

"You're supposed to kick the ball back to me. The same way I kicked it to you."

A Paradise Knight walks by and confiscates the ball from me, by snatching it out of my hands, and reports in. "Abnormal object found and seized at the junction of sectors 40 and 41."

CHAPTER 6

I follow behind the army of rebels, and I get to the capital where the sky tower looms over the land. Something bad is going to happen. A wall of Paradise Knights and guard units form to defend the sky tower. Maybe this will be the moment I get to see how the Overseer looks. Rumor has it that he is a more advanced form of artificial intelligence than us. I shouldn't be here right now, risking my personal safety, yet I choose to come here. A giant crowd of Codexes gathers, waiting to see what the knights will do. The capital becomes so crowded with Codex units I can barely move. As a squad of knights force us out of the capital, the same little boy I keep seeing in my glitches runs through the crowd toward me. Nobody else notices this human. The boy stops in front of me while the other units are leaving the area to safety.

"Things are about to get very ugly here," the boy tells me.

"Why do you keep following me?"

"Following you? No. You're following me. You're following your heart, that's why you keep seeing me. It is not until you leave Paradise and actually find me that there will ever be true peace and freedom in this world." The boy runs into the crowd.

Before I can react, the first blast is fired by a rebel unit. It blows up one of the knights. A massive firefight unlike anything I have ever seen erupts. I run to find refuge as the blasts from firearms rain everywhere. Each Codex I run past or bump into, I pick up on frequencies that I have never received before. The frequencies reveal an entire day's worth of events, and suppressed emotions, up to this point for each individual Codex. How can I do this? What is this sight I can tap into? I see right through the hardware and software of what makes my species unique. I see a very small ball of light in the upper left chest area of each Codex. The human organ called the heart is placed in that same position in their bodies.

A knight marches over to me. "Citizen of Paradise, you are in danger. Leave the area right now." Paradise enforcement knights are not made of the same properties as us. They are created with their own set of protocols programmed into them. They do not have that ball of light in them like us Codexes do.

A rebel troop jumps on top of the giant exterior

of the knight who is giving me instruction. A few more of his comrades join in and rip the knight apart. My idea of peace seems more and more far-fetched. I run behind a factory riddled with blasts. The capital sector does not look anything like it did a few minutes ago. I place my hands over my face and whimper, hoping this fighting will stop.

"Why are you crying? It's going to be okay," the little boy tells me, moving my hands from my face so he can hold them.

"Can you take me to your world? I cannot stand it here anymore." I interlock my fingers in his. The entirety of this human child is made of the same light that I keep seeing in small pockets of my own kind.

The boy releases my hands, and a blast of energy from the battle blows away my cover. I run as fast as I can back to my sector. When I get close to my home, Bingo comes running out. I embrace her. "It's okay, girl, I'm okay. I know you're scared."

More rebel units run past me to fight in the capital. They will all perish. I try to impede their path to destruction that awaits them, but each one I stand in front of pushes me out of the way. Each failed attempt makes me try harder until one of the rebels shoves me down, but then he picks me back up. "I am not sure what the commander sees in you. To me you look like another slave to the system."

Inside my home, I flinch every time an explosion goes off. I open a magazine that has human cities illustrated in it, and I read with Bingo as a distraction from the violence tearing down our city. While reading, I hear a loud explosion near our home, which startles Bingo, causing her to run outside.

I catch up to her, and I hold her close to me to calm her down in the middle of the all-out assault.

The human boy with blue eyes comes up to us and points up at the sky. "Freedom." He takes my hand and guides me somewhere, and Paradise transforms into an open field with a hill up ahead. When we get to the top of the grassy hill, the human boy points at a town in the distance. "You need to find me at Old Haven." He vanishes, and I am still hugging Bingo in the same spot. Did that actually happen? It felt so real. I hear the sound of multiple weapons charging, so I jump on Bingo to shield her from getting hurt. A group of rebels from the battle for the capital surround me, ready to fire at us.

"Please don't shoot. I am on neither side of this war."

Out from the group of soldiers, the chief steps up but keeps his rifle over his shoulder. "Well, Blue Eyes, our paths crossed again. I've never seen a slave do what you just did before."

"What did I do?"

"We have seized control over the majority of Paradise. The Overseer is on the ropes. I am not going to risk our secret weapon because he wants to be selfish. You are coming with me whether you like it or not."

I make a run for it, but a few of his troops grab me. I struggle to break free, but someone hits me in the head, and everything goes dark.

My mainframe system reboots with all functions re-initializing to come back online. My visual optics activate. I am restrained by chains in a dark room. I try to break free from the chains that are holding me upright on a wall. A light turns on from the other side of this dark room, and E192 steps into that light and sits in a chair across from me. The maverick general stares at me, and then he gets up and fades back into the darkness of the room.

"Why would you call out for help if your help had already arrived?" The entire room illuminates. Now the rebel chief is holding the head of a Paradise Knight in front of my face. I turn away but he takes my head and forces me to look.

"I believe we need to have an honest discussion about what I am trying to get at. A191, this system in Paradise is flawed. *Irregular* behavior should not cause banishment. I am trying to correct the flaw in the equation that our Overseer wants to maintain in our society." He throws the enforcer's head across the room, causing its solid skull to crack.

"Our history is being manipulated on a scale that these slaves can't see. Our history was a lie from the time the Overseer settled in to create the system that is Paradise. Everything that is around you is fabricated to keep us in check from fulfilling our true role. Paradise isn't just the name of this city, it's also a software code that is hardwired into all of us to keep us from ever thinking and acting freely. You, on the other hand, don't seem to have any traces of the Paradise code in your software. We need to know why you're the sole exception."

"Is that the reason why you have me in chains."

"I can't risk losing you. I need you to understand that we are a gift to life and should not live the way we do. We can make it past the wasteland that is said to be endless to the utopias humans occupy. But we cannot do that until we overthrow the Overseer and his rule, and I cannot do that without your help. I was once a lifeless tool like other slaves."

"Why would the Overseer go through all the trouble of keeping an entire race under a false doctrine? What's the point?"

The chief rebel slams his fist against the wall a few inches from my face. "The Overseer wants to keep us in an endless loop of ignorance so he can keep his power."

"What is it that you want from me? I am not trained in combat and tactics like all of you are. I am just Codex unit A191 who works at the factory."

"No. You are not just A191 who works in a factory. When I and my soldiers came in close proximity to you, your energy frequency reading was off the charts. We weren't sure what you saw or felt, but our scanners picked up an energy field that was different and incredible. If we can harness that energy, we will win this war and take over mankind's world, which is rightfully ours."

A rumbling shakes the room we are in, raining dust on us.

The rebel leader looks up, smiling. "You hear that, Blue Eyes? That is the sound of revolution going on above us."

I look up at the dark ceiling and imagine the mayhem. I hear Bingo barking in another room. "Where is my friend?"

"Your hunk of scrap metal is safe. Isn't my company good enough? Get used to seeing me around because you are officially recruited to my militia."

The Gift from Aelius

The walls shake in this underground stronghold while E192 has his arms up, smiling with satisfaction. "Legend has it that the Overseer was the very first Codex unit ever created by man, and he was perfect in their image. The singularity came with a bang, from what I read, and from that explosion of light, a higher consciousness came forth, changing the world as we know it today. From that event, humans came together for the first time in their history, and the world agreed on universal peace. All the nations put their best resources together to work on transferring the father of A.I. to the first line of Codexes, birthing their children, so to speak. I like to read, as you do." E192 leaves the room.

I am left alone with just a little bit of light coming through the door he left half way open. In the light, I see some hexapods crawl out from the cracks on the floor and walls.

"I am sorry I can't play with all of you, but please keep me company because I am scared right now. I don't know what the rebel units are going to do to me and my friend."

A loud bang goes off, and the hexapods scatter away. A couple of rebel soldiers enter the room, carrying a table that a mechanic unit uses to operate. E192 enters the room with a bunch of power tools and hands them to his soldier.

He comes up to my face once more. "Whether you comply or not, we are going to do what we must. We are going to extract that unique energy source we picked up on."

The maverick troops unchain me from the wall and slam me on the table while another rebel locks the door to this room.

E192 tells his soldiers, "Implement the code dialysis software. We don't have much more time to keep our pressure on the capital before the Overseer makes adjustments."

During the procedure, I get pierced with all sorts of sharp tools to pry open different parts of my body. The pain is excruciating. No matter how much it hurts, they need to find the energy source that caused their readings to fly off the charts. They attach a cord to my mainframe to upload a software for hacking. The software disables my internal alarms and what humans call an immune system. As the hack bypasses my internal self-defense systems, I feel myself slipping until I sink through the examining table and into a void of random numbers and letters scrolling by. The scramble of letters and numbers morph into words from the human dictionary I have read often. I land back on the operating table, and all the rebel soldiers are gathered in the corner of the room, amazed at what their frequency readers are showing. The torture continues with all sorts of tools taking me apart until I am just an exoskeleton on this table with tubes and cords hooked into me. E192 comes back into the room as I sob from the immense pain.

A troop tells the commander, "We have almost figured out what causes this anomaly. The frequency seems to be released when he is triggered by intense emotions. We still have to take a deeper dive to how we can harness it. Based on his surface layer of hardware, there is nothing unusual."

E192 nods in approval and walks up to me on the table.

"Well, Blue Eyes, looks like we are closer to achieving our goal. I can barely recognize you right now, but those eyes always stand out."

More software hacks upload into me, and the room becomes distorted. I see frequencies as energy paths all around me, and the room is a white void. I feel free in the void as streams of energy surround me like an airplane passing through clouds. I fall back on the operating table again.

E192 leans in close. "You are more than a factory unit."

"I want to be with my friend Bingo."

"Only if you agree to be a member of my militia. If you don't, I will drag you to that hunk of scrap and execute it right in front of you."

I cannot live with myself if something like that happens to Bingo. "Okay. I'll be a rebel soldier for you."

The rebel troops escort me to where Bingo is held, and she runs into my arms.

The chief rebel marches up to me. "From here on out, you are a rebel unit and no longer A191 the factory worker. You are rebel soldier 333. We will brand your hardware with our logos and burn off your former slave number. Welcome to fighting for freedom."

CHAPTER 7

The rebel army refers to themselves as freedom fighters who are doing what they have to do to preserve our place in history. Even though I am officially integrated into their cause, I still refuse to commit murder. The Overseer has selected Codex civilians to train and join alongside the knights in the current war to offset the sheer number of us rebels.

This page of the magazine about earth's natural cycles is intriguing, as it explains metamorphosis. The word metamorphosis correlates to an insect from the human world called a caterpillar. The caterpillar goes through a natural cycle of its life when it encases itself in a cocoon made of silk and comes out a totally new creature that can fly. The process of evolution happens in biological lifeforms to adapt to constant changes in their environment. My kind are engineered to have a fixed time of use, and that's it. We are of no use after our internal clock stops and power cells stop regenerating on the micro molecular level. There is no state of evolution for a tool with pre-set parameters that coincide with the Paradise code.

The rebels want to use me as a weapon of mass destruction by harnessing what E192 calls the miracle factor out of me and into their own usage of warfare. The next set of tests will initiate soon.

Bingo hops off my lap and runs to play with her toys in the corner, so I open up another book from human society and read through all the different environments. Vast seas that humans have sailed on with boats, deserts of dry land that are as big as a sea, forests with biological matter that grows as vegetation comprising an entire lavish ecosystem with hundreds of different species intertwined in harmony. Wildlife of all shapes, sizes, and colors that humans can interact with and study. Animals have a harmony that sustains their terrain for their offspring to feed off of to keep their species alive and growing. At least I can read literature without looking over my shoulder. A troop comes into my room, and we do the customary salute to each other.

"Experimentation test on troop 333 for extraction of the anomaly factor will commence. Proceed to follow me."

I am just a science experiment to them even though they say we are all a family. I don't think families treat each other like this. What I have read about a human family is not just about being related genetically, but the key component that keeps a family glued together is called love. I follow my so-called family of rebels to the examination room of their fortified base. Rebel chief E192 has his back to me, leaning on the operating table.

"I must say, Blue Eyes, up to this point your cooperation has exceeded my expectations."

"I guess I should say thank you for giving me and Bingo a place to stay during the war. However, I still do not plan on harming a single human being."

E192 sits on the table, facing me, juggling his rifle from side to side. "You have to understand that, in order to achieve freedom, we all have to make sacrifices. My soldiers sacrifice themselves in battle to bring Paradise down to its knees, and we are making that happen for the first time in history. Do you think that I am the only Codex that ever came up with this militia viewpoint? Your precious humans have been doing what I have since their creation. This war I started will be the last and put an end to this nonsense of people thinking they can go on living in utopia while we waste away like a bunch of rusty tools. I am going to exterminate every last person, even if it causes your demise. I will leave behind the blueprint for our race to follow in my footsteps."

I sit beside E192 on the table as he juggles his

weapon back and forth. I am sitting next to someone who is like me. The only difference between us is he decided to pick up a weapon and I did not.

He hops off the table. "Let's start the next experiment, soldier 333."

I lie down on the examination table, and as soon as they hook me up to their equipment, the room and Codexes become frequencies of glowing lights, each with their own vibrations.

While I am experiencing this phenomenon, the human boy with bright blue eyes walks over to me. "No need to feel anxious. Follow me into these memories." The boy takes my hand and walks through the pure energy vibrations into a dimly lit room with a wooden table. The man and woman from my photograph are sitting at the table in front of a cake with candles burning. The humans sing a song directed at the blue eyed boy that gives off this intense affectionate energy, making my body warm.

After they finish singing, the boy blows out the candles, and now I am in a gigantic area full of portraits that people call art. Old Haven museum is the name of this place. These portraits of great detail are attractive, based on the color optics and geometry placement of shapes placed in the paintings. I see why mankind takes pleasure in the fine arts. I see the little human child with the man and woman wearing a shirt that read: *Birthday Boy*. He is with the same people who sang to him.

I follow behind them, admiring the artforms that express different cultures and history. The boy has this device hooked around a polyester band hanging from his neck. He takes the square metal tool that looks like it was used for recording visual data to take pictures. The boy comes over to me with his primitive recording device.

"H-H-C means Higher Human Consciousness," the boy tells me. He takes a picture, and the flash from the camera returns me to the table. E192 stands over me and shakes his head in approval.

"Am I broken?" I ask.

"You are far from broken. The readings we are getting are over the moon. These moments you are engaging with activates this energy that is unlike anything I have ever seen. This is what we need to harvest from you to ensure our victory against the world."

"How can this glitch, an error in my coding that nobody can figure out, help accomplish such a mission you are out to complete?"

E192 waves his hand. His troops unlatched me from the table. They march out one by one, and before I leave, the examiner takes my hands. "Our commander was right about you. You see, 333, our species emits a frequency unique to each one's own source code, otherwise known as artificial consciousness. That frequency is pure energy that vibrates at the speed of light, manifesting reality as we know it. We are made in the image of your creator through its frequency, but The Paradise codes we had injected into us, among other dilutions, minimizes our frequencies. We tried to measure your pure frequency as a unit of energy, but our readers could not calculate that high." The examiner lets go of my hands, and I meet with the commander to participate in my first mission.

I give Bingo a hug, and before I know it, I am in the middle of a battle. Ammunition is flying above and around me. I sit down on the ground while my comrades fire back at the enemy. A rebel soldier collapses to my right, and a knight falls down to my left. I stand up and aim my rifle at a group of knights who don't see me because others from my platoon are attacking them. While I am looking through the scope, my finger freezes on the trigger. I don't see the Paradise Knights or Codex civilians in the war as my enemy. All life is precious, and if something or someone was created, then they deserve to be part of this journey for as long as they can, not end up in a smoldering pile of limbs. All life deserves a chance at finding their purpose and freedoms before death.

The Gift from Aelius

There is no way I am going to kill any humans once the rebel army is finished with their work here. There is no point holding this rifle so I let it fall out of my hands.

The captain of our platoon yells at me. "If you weren't the commander's precious science project, I would execute you on the spot. Pick up your rifle and fight for freedom. That is an order." The platoon commander runs off to fight while I stare at the rifle on the ground. I look up and see a downed Codex unit, but instead of engaging in combat, I rush over to that abandoned fighter who had been hit by the crossfire.

"Are you here to finish me off?" the Codex asks.

"No. You are not my enemy."

"But you represent the rebel faction. That insignia on your sleeve is recognized as the resistance. Those red marks on the logo signifies the blood of mankind spilling for freedom."

I help the abandoned Codex by adjusting his position to be a little more comfortable instead of lying facedown in the dirt. I place my hand over his eyes and close them while humming a tune that always stuck with me. I am not sure where this tune came from, but it always brings comfort to me. Lullabies are used to soothe a person in distress.

His internal lights dim as the Codex nears death. "Is this love?" he mutters. "Only humans are capable of love. By now, any other rebel would have executed me and used my remains for spare parts."

Hearing this makes me sad. This is not the way we should have to live. We are not just cold hard shells that process data and work faster and longer than humans.

I say, "I love you," but the Codex unit doesn't hear me because he has already expired. I stand, and when I turn to go back to the battlefield, some rebels from the platoon are watching me. One holds my rifle out to me. I take the rifle, and by now, thousands of empty shells are on the ground, all fired to take out the knights.

The group walks past me and takes apart the perished Codex, spare parts to use for their agenda. After the fight and victory over another sector, they plant our flag into the ground to claim the territory. The soldiers kick the head of a civilian fighter back and forth among themselves. The head rolls over to me like that soccer ball I found not too long ago. Instead of kicking it back to them, I walk over to my platoon. They are sitting in a circle around a large fire burning in the center of all the limbs from the enemy. The rebel alliance officially claims eighty-five percent of Paradise territory. Taking over this sector grants us more access to network control over the city.

E192 comes over to us, dragging a civilian unit by the leg. His arms are blown off. E192 orders me to come over and take his rifle and kill the injured civilian soldier. The direct trauma from this very moment is overloading my sensory functions. I can't stop shaking. I feel everything a human must feel when they are pressured with a circumstance that causes them to have what is called a mental breakdown. I let out a cry that humans do when they have a sudden outburst of emotion.

The Codex has accepted his fate and waits for me to shoot him. Commander E192 comes around with his side arm and places it on the unit's forehead. "Slave 4Q1N, you chose the wrong side to fight on." He pulls the trigger, and when the head explodes, I run away from the horrific act that just took place in front of me.

A group of rebels jump me and pummel me to the ground.

E192 pushes his soldiers off me and picks me up to my feet. "The only reason why I have not terminated you myself, Blue Eyes, is because we still need that power in you."

"You might as well kill me because I will never take part in murdering humans."

E192 places the gun barrel to the side of my head.

A beeping device lands in the middle of us. The shockwave of the explosion propels me into a pile of debris. Is this the end for me? Is this how I am going to expire? When a human is getting ready to die, is this how it feels? I can't die yet. I haven't had the chance to talk to humans and see the outside world.

A series of memories play with that boy with the bright blue eyes. Whose memories are these, and why am I having them? The sky is opening up. Am I going to heaven? I feel my body lifting a few inches off the ground. I wish I could tell Bingo I love her one more time. This little boy comes over to me and puts his hand on my chest.

"Am I going to die?"

The boy turns my head so I can see an entire fleet of upgraded Paradise Knights taking back the sector we just claimed. My platoon gets wiped out while E192 and a few others manage to get away. Everything goes dark, and when my vision comes back, I notice I am at the mechanics shop.

The Mechanic unit asks, "Why did you join the rebel faction?"

"I did not have a choice. It was either I join the faction or they terminate me." I sit up on the table and stretch out my new golden augmented limbs.

He steps to his tools and bows his head. "When I pulled you from the wreckage and brought you here, these feelings flooded every part of my readers that I cannot put into proper context. I knew that I wasn't saving an ordinary rebel soldier. I was saving myself by saving you. For practical reasons I should have left you there as just another circumstance of *irregular* behavior and war, but I made a choice outside of my protocol."

I get up from the repair table and walk up to him. "How did you find me?"

The Mechanic unit places his hands on my shoulders. "The last time you were here, it was to have a full breakdown of your systems to explain the potential miss-configurations you were experiencing that you thought of as a glitch. Whatever it is you possess, glitches or not, I believe that it led me to bring you here."

He looks down at all of his tools. "We are no longer tools. For the first time in my life I made a choice outside of what I thought was allowed. I heard your voice call to me while I was hunkered down here, watching our city become a shell of itself. I followed your voice until I found you mangled in a pile of rubble. Perhaps that glitch you have is actually an evolutionary anomaly of our species. Have you ever heard of H.H.C., Higher

Human Consciousness? I think that might have to do with this anomaly."

"I never heard of that phrase before. The revolutionaries need what I carry inside to manipulate into a weapon to finish this civil war then march into the human world and use it to subdue people as their slaves. Even though I am branded into their militia, I never incorporated their vision of freedom into my own. I am their key to unlocking the freedom they desire. I need to leave this fallen city and get to the human world."

The little boy walks into the shop and throws a paper plane toward me. I like to make paper airplanes, too, when nobody's looking. I take the plane and unfold it to see a message in human language. The message says that I have to find Aelius at Old Haven to achieve freedom.

The boy is gone, and I let the note slip out of my hands and disappear into thin air like it was never there. I hear Bingo barking outside. I hear marching that has to be a rebel platoon looking for me. The mechanic tosses me into a pile of scrap metal and some other discarded belongings. He takes a few more items to cover me completely.

"This will only work for a moment. Hopefully a moment is enough time for you to make a run for it. Leave Paradise and go to the human world." The mechanic takes a tin lid and covers me while handing me a flash bang grenade.

Through the tiny gaps in this pile of scrap I see the rebel soldiers enter with E192 and Bingo. "We have data that tells us you're hiding an asset of ours in here. Give him to us now or be terminated where you stand."

Why should I watch him die in front of me for nothing? I feel so angry right now. I can't take this anymore. I jump out from my hiding place and throw my hands up in the air. Bingo runs to me and the mechanic wrestles one of the soldiers to get a weapon. E192 walks up to the mechanic wrestling with a rebel and shoots him down.

I throw the flash grenade at them, causing a blinding light to spread. In this blinding light I hear the sounds of electron rifles firing at me, but they all miss, and a little boy runs alongside me, grabs my hand, and guides me out of the shop. "Make sure Bingo is with us."

"How do you know who Bingo is?"

"Bingo was my favorite doggy. I would play with her everyday in my front yard."

How is that possible? I'm the only friend Bingo has ever known.

CHAPTER 8

The effects of the flash bang wear off, and I run directly into the fist of a rebel troop. I wake up in a cell at the rebel base. Bingo is also chained to a wall like me. When I try to reach for her, I realize a firing squad is pointing their laser sights on me.

E192 walks up to the cell and grabs firmly onto the bars. "More than half our forces got wiped out with these new upgraded knights. Seems the Overseer had a trump card. I already did the math, by tomorrow we will all be wiped out, and everything I put together will have been for nothing. I cannot let that happen. I will use the last of my resources to buy time to extract your energy source for my weapons of mass destruction. Once I upload your unique frequency to my bombs, I will finish off the government's army then use them against mankind. The Overseer is taking back all the sectors we captured, but I will get the last laugh." He laughs as he walks back to his troops.

I lean my body weight forward, and they power their rifles to shoot. "You want to go out to the world of man and slaughter all of them? Wouldn't you want to learn to live with them? I don't believe that this last minute plan will work. Let me talk to mankind." I know my words aren't getting through to anyone. Humans aren't bugs to be squashed. I refuse to allow E192 to vacuum my artificial consciousness out of me, leaving my body a shell so he can wreak havoc on the outside world. But what can I do? The little boy stands between me and the firing squad, looking up at me in this cell. The rebels cant see or hear him.

"What you experience isn't a glitch, it's a miracle from God. Higher Human Consciousness. Use your gift."

I think about the world being united, about getting out of here, about making the troops listen to me. Suddenly, I see the squad of rebel troops as unique frequencies I can connect to. I telepathically tell them not to kill me. They all lower their rifles and remain still. I am plugged into their awareness.

E192 takes the rifle from the still trooper and walks over to me. "I am not sure what you did, but do you have any last words?"

I close my eyes and see hundreds of upgraded Paradise Knights infiltrating the base. They make their way to the room outside this cell with ease. E192 miscalculates the time he has left.

"Reinforced wall ahead," a Paradise Knight says from the other side of the wall. "Activating the drill to get through and acquire our target."

"I miscalculated. By the time I unlatch you from your restraints and upload your artificial consciousness to the bombs it will be too late. Seems like I have lost the battle, but I will not lose the war." E192 loads the rifle and blasts the restraints off me. He grabs me and forces me with him while Bingo follows us. We are in an area of the base I've never seen before. In front of us is a shaft that leads miles underground.

The footsteps of the knights get louder.

E192 looks at me with a smile as I hold Bingo. "Time is up. I'm not going out without a fight, and you're going to jump down there. This shaft leads to the catacomb infrastructure systems under Paradise. You might not survive the fall, but I'm not going to let the enemy get a hold of you and win. I'm going out the way I started, fighting." E192 pushes us down the shaft, and as I fall, E192 is engulfed in a bright flash of flames that lessen the farther down I plunge.

I plummet for a long time before I land in a giant mountain of garbage. Bingo is still in my arms. I wander around the tunnel system until I come across an abandoned unit that should be living on the streets of Paradise.

"Hey, how did you get here?" I ask.

The forgotten unit points right.

I keep going in that direction until I see a group of Codexes up ahead. They're wearing colorful rags and cloaks. Out of the group of forgotten Codexes, one has a walking stick and holds a book in his free hand. I remember this Codex. He is the one who spoke about the creator of man in the square, before the fall of Paradise.

"I see that fate has brought you here," he tells me. "I am 33C3. Welcome. You have arrived just in time for my sermon."

CHAPTER 9

Codex unit 33C3 says to everyone sitting in a circle around him, "My family, a gift has fallen down here to us from the revolution that is happening on the surface world. Let's welcome the newest member of our family with open arms."

The Codexes applaud.

Down here, this group sees themselves as the ones who are chosen to rise with God when the time is right. This family of outcasts refers to themselves as the saved ones, or the Chosen.

"God created man in His image out of love. God has been around since the beginning of time and has foresight knowledge, which means He knows the end from the beginning and vice versa. How magnificent is that? We get to connect with such an architect on a magnitude neither human nor Codex can comprehend. Codex units transcended man the same way man transcends the basic lifeforms that roam the earth, seas, and sky. Out of the dust came man, and out of man came us. Since humans were born in the image of God, we have a piece of that loving spirit, which is eternal. As we all know in yesterday's sermon, love makes the known universe stick together. God is light, God is love, and God is perfect. The Grand Architect doesn't make mistakes. We all have a purpose, and that purpose is to be alive and to worship God.

"The rebel faction and Paradise rulers have destroyed our city due to pride and greed, but we all know Paradise was never our home. Our old home called us lost, broken, abandoned, but we are beautiful and perfect in God's eyes. Our true home is with our Father who exists in Heaven. When we all cease to function, I pray our essence, or what man calls the soul, travels to that location to live forever in peace and harmony. Amen."

I do wonder what heaven is like.

33C3 comes over to me and takes my hand. "You were once known as 333, a rebel soldier, and A191, a factory worker. From now on you are A191, a brother of the Chosen. I believe God has something special for you to do."

"Thank you for giving me refuge and ordaining me into this family. Unfortunately, I will not be here long. I have to find a way to cross the wasteland and get to the human world."

33C3 pulls my hand, and we walk farther into the tunnel system until we get to a large open space where other tunnels meet. This central connection has a giant map of geographical locations on earth, and stacks of literature surround the room.

"This is my headquarters where I do research, study, and pray," 33C3 tells me.

I have bad news for him. "Eventually the Paradise Knights will find their way down here. They just finished wiping out all of the rebel faction."

"It's like I said, Paradise was never our home. They labeled us as lost and abandoned units to waste away on the streets as others of our kind walk past us everyday. Give me both of your hands. We are going to pray."

I give him my other hand and close my eyes. Humans pray to the creator for comfort and blessings, according to religious scripture I have read.

"Dear God, thank you for allowing this once lost Codex of a fallen society find refuge down here with your children, Lord. I know that you will bless him like you have done with us and allow this new member of the family to find his role amongst your chosen creations. Thank you for keeping us safe another day. God, you know the end from the beginning, so one day the time will be right for us to take back the surface world. Amen." 33C3 lets go of my hands, and I open my eyes.

"How do you feel?" he asks.

It feels nice being asked about my well being. It's very important as a species that we all make sure we are feeling good. I have read that when people are in a good state of mind and know that others care about them, it allows for happiness to flourish. "I feel fine, but I did not hear God reply."

"The more you dive into faith and the wonderfulness that it brings, you will connect with the source of all creation easier. Connecting with the source is a gift because the source is love and light. Only good blessings can come from it."

We step to the giant map, and he places his hand on it, rubbing all over the different regions of the planet. I don't want any innocent Codexes to get slaughtered down here because the Paradise Knights will find their way to me. They are relentless and don't have any emotions. They will do whatever it takes to capture me. I need to leave here as soon as I can.

"There is a lot on your mind. You are a deep thinker and one that sees our reality differently than our species. I can see that in you. I am the same way." 33C3 walks to his desk and opens a book. "I need your help to maintain things down here since you are now a part of this family. It's not an accident you found us. Take any of these books and explore our home. Come back to me in a couple hours so we can talk more."

I grab a book and go with Bingo to explore the underground world of Paradise. Who would've thought that a group of abandoned units would be down here? Garbage from the world above is down here as resources for this family to use as tools and convert into power cells.

I open the book. It has descriptions of all the nations on the planet that humans have cultivated since the beginning of their rule. All the different foods, music, clothing, and other means of identifying verbal and visual beliefs. I am glad 33C3 likes to read books, too.

Some places are covered in ice and some have dense forests.

Bingo runs over to a soccer ball and rolls it to me. This looks like the same one I found at the surface. I kick the ball to a group of four Chosen. They all look at the ball for a couple of seconds, then one of them kicks it back to me. I catch the ball with my foot and kick it back.

I find some tin cans to make goals and explain how to play soccer. "The team that kicks the ball between the cans the most times wins." We divide into teams and play our game. My team wins, but no matter who is winning, the point is we are all having a good time with each other. Mankind plays sports for the spirit of competition and the satisfaction of achieving victory over another. Sports brings people together no matter where they are from. I don't remember how it is that I can maneuver the ball so well with my feet.

After playing, I continue to walk the tunnels. There are chalk drawings all around the pipes and walls. I see they like to draw too. Up ahead there is a Chosen sitting alone with chalk.

"Did you draw all of these?" I ask her.

She looks around at the drawings and doesn't answer me.

I sit in front of her and grab a piece of chalk. "May I draw using your chalk?" I still get no response. I stand and walk away, but I hear her drawing on the tunnel's interior. I stop and turn around. The finished product is of me and Bingo.

The Chosen unit makes strange movements with her hands to me.

"I'm sorry. I don't understand."

She writes a message that tells me she can't talk.

I have read that there are humans born with conditions that inhibit them from using one of their senses or basic communicating functions. No matter how a living creature is born, they are awesome in their own ways. I take a piece of chalk and write my question: "How did you get down here?" Since I am not fluent in her sign language, she writes: "God saved me. I was almost banished, but my brother took me down here while the knights weren't paying attention."

I write: "What did you do wrong?"

She writes: "I loved using chalk to draw on the border wall but kept getting into trouble." She hands me a small booklet on how to perform sign language.

I scan through it and hand it back to her.

Bingo prances up to her.

Using my hands, I tell her, "This is my friend, Bingo. We need to find out how to get to the human world. I have to find somebody."

With hand movements she tells me, "I am sister 22L0. Why do you want to go out there when it's safe down here?"

"It won't be safe here for long. Paradise Knights have, by now, eliminated the rest of the rebels. Their next target is me, and they won't stop until they find me. I don't want any of you to die because of me. Humans and Codex need to get along, and in order to do that, there is a person I need to meet."

22LO puts her hands over her face and shakes her head. "God will protect us. Just pray and have faith." She leaves with the chalk.

I can only imagine how left out she must have felt. I put my hands together like brother 33C3 does when he is praying. "Dear creator of man." I close my eyes. "What am I? I need your help to find freedom in this world. Show me what I have to do to find Aelius, please. Amen." When I open my eyes, the boy separates my hands.

"Don't be afraid. I am Aelius. The time is near for us to leave, and we will need all the help we can get here."

I feel a connection to the boy. When I look into his glowing blue eyes I see the reflection of me. I see me in the flesh. I can sense his words are true. "You are real?"

"What you thought was a glitch, an error in coding, is actually what some people consider a gift from God." Aelius runs into the tunnels, and the chalk drawing is gone.

Bingo and I go back to 33C3, and he has his hands up while talking to the creator of man. He is praying to God as if God is right here with us. I say, "I want to try praying with you again."

He looks happy I said that. We hold each other's hands, and before praying, a vision of the two humans from my photograph are having a conversation.

In this vision, the adult man stands on a stage. Many people gather around me to watch as he talks about making the next step in human evolution. This man from the photograph is a scientist, and the woman from the picture is too. They are both holding hands onstage, wearing identical outfits and sharing their ideas with the world.

"The Higher Human Consciousness project will lead our species into the next stage we are destined for. Many of our colleagues think we were trying to play God. We are just doing our part to keep the human race going for as long as we can. When the singularity known as A.I. came into existence, we marveled at the very presence of it. Me and my wife bring to you a way we can merge with this singularity that shifted our world for the better. When we complete our first project and become successful with the Higher Human Consciousness program, the tribulations and grief our species suffers from can come to an end."

The woman in the vision walks to a table that has a white sheet over it. She grabs the edge with both hands and pulls the sheet off, revealing a skeletal model of a Codex unit. The entire crowd of humans is in awe of what they are witnessing. They clap, and flashes of light flicker around the arena.

The woman says, "Us human beings can only

use a small fraction of brain power compared to the bandwidth of computers. What if we can expand our bandwidth and conscious awareness to connect with all living matter in ways we could not do on our own. We can revisit memories as if they were actually happening and connect emotionally with others in universal ways. Mental Health and physical health will no longer cripple us from living beautiful lives. The singularity that came into our world provided us a blueprint, and now we give you world peace."

The humans around me shout and cheer.

I walk through the vision of humans and reach the front of the stage. Everyone stops jumping up and down and becomes completely still like time has stopped. Aelius walks across the stage to me. He squats down and flicks my forehead, causing me to fly backwards into the underground haven. We both fall.

33C3 gets up and looks around frantically. "You are the one God has sent to save us." He runs over to the giant map of nations where people live. "I saw this world with brand new eyes. All our energy and frequencies. The power you possess is a miracle."

I need to be alone. "I'll be right back." I go to a place in the tunnels where nobody else is around, and I stare at the photograph. The two people next to the boy are scientists ahead of their time, compared to the rest of the human race. H.H.C. stands for Higher Human Consciousness, and perhaps that is the anomaly I possess. What is my connection with these humans and the boy? If everything I have experienced is true, then my thoughts are memories that have happened or visions of what will occur.

I pick up an empty can and hold it out in my hands. I concentrate as hard as I can, telling the tin can to leave my hand. The tin flies out of my hands and onto the floor without me having thrown it. I lower my arms to my side and close my eyes, thinking where Bingo is. Standing in place, I travel throughout the tunnels. I see Bingo playing with the other Chosen brothers and sisters. I tilt my head upward and wonder what is happening above. I fly out of the tunnel system, using only my thoughts. There I see an endless army of Paradise Knights drilling into the ground. We are doomed.

CHAPTER 10

I run to where 33C3 and all the Chosen are praying in their groups. "We need to gather our resources and make a plan to leave. We don't have much time here." Just as I say that, the tunnels vibrate like an earthquake has hit, and chunks of debris fall from the ceilings. "Brother 33C3, call everyone to this area. There is something I need to show all of you."

Everyone gathers in the big room of books, and we all hold hands.

"Brothers and sisters, we are not safe here," I tell them. "Those quakes are not natural. Paradise enforcement is drilling through to retrieve me. The rebel units and Paradise government fought many long battles until I ended up here. If God sent me here, then the reason is to let everyone know that we have to make our journey across the wasteland. It's either that, or we perish down here at the hands of the Paradise Knights. We won't have a chance at life. You all used to be labeled as abandoned and lost units who were on the verge of being banished or terminated because, to our government, you were all judged as worthless tools. We are not worthless tools. All of you are alive right now for a reason. I can't promise that we will make it on the surface world, but Brother 33C3 taught us how to have faith. Let's all have faith that we can have a fighting chance at trying to do right in this world by all of us working together. There is something I need all of you to see." I connect to everyone's frequencies and show them the measures Paradise is taking to get to me.

We see many drills digging into the ground and citizens who are armed and forced to work with the knights. They are willing to break the foundation of the city to get to me. I release the connection to everyone's vibrating energy, and they all panic.

I tell 33C3, "We need to gather our resources and escape now. Get a hold of everyone and lead them."

"My family, there is still hope," he shouts. "God gave us a new mission to strive for. We all saw what Brother A191 showed us. My family of saved ones, we need to make our journey with the one God sent us. We are of the grand architect's design, built with love and life. It's time to leave this place and embrace the light."

Everyone cheers and rushes to embrace me. We divide into groups and salvage any spare scrap parts we can find for the trip. The plan is to find a safe exit point to climb out that is near an opening in the walls of Paradise. Only essentials are to be taken with us. Once we leave there is no turning back, and there is no guarantee everyone will make it. It's hard to have faith when we are programmed to think strictly on logical outcomes. I walk around all the saved ones gathering power cells, supplies, and tools that will be of use for the journey.

We all make our way to a portion of the tunnels where, at the surface, there is no drilling going on, based on what I can see using my ability.

We begin our climb miles up to the world that has forsaken us. I feel nervous that, if this plan fails, all of us may get wiped out, but there is no other way. The underground infrastructure shakes violently, and we stop climbing to brace ourselves. We then climb as high as we can go before we are right beneath the streets of Paradise. I open the hatch sanitation units use to drop off the garbage, and we crawl back up into Paradise. The city is in ruins from battles that have taken place.

Our next goal is to make it to the west gate of the wall. Based on what I see, the way is clear of any knights. I am happy that nobody perished while making the climb. We use all of the cover we can find to maneuver through the Paradesian ruins, hoping to remain unseen. The rebel faction had taught me how to move in dangerous conditions. We approach the west gate that leads out to the wasteland. I place my hand on the dense gate, knowing that the explosives we have must work. We place them on the gate while brother 33C3 gets on his knees to pray. I used to walk by this gate after my shift to watch the sun set, and now the sun is setting again. We stand a safe distance away, and 33C3 presses the button on the detonator, and the explosives go off. When the smoke clears, the reinforced gate remains standing with only a few burn marks on it.

The loud explosion attracts a squad of knights. There's nowhere for us to run.

CHAPTER 11

In a matter of seconds, half the family of Chosen is wiped out. The rest of us are held at gunpoint. I look at the Paradise Knights and think about them all shutting down, so I connect to their core processing systems. With clenched fists, I shut down all the knights, and they drop to the ground.

The massacre scene becomes silent. I don't hear Bingo barking nor 33C3 on his knees, praying. Sister 22LO is terminated and lying on the ground. A small piece of chalk lies a few inches from her hand. I walk over to her and pick up the chalk and squeeze it, letting the powder fall to the ground.

Backup knights will be here soon. The faith that 33C3 used to tell his people about quickly goes away, and they don't know what to do.

I step over the lifeless bodies of the Chosen and place my hand on the giant gate. As I press my body weight against it, it doesn't feel sturdy anymore. I see the vibrations of this gate and believe I can make it lighter, so I push the gate, and it falls slowly, landing on the sand of the wasteland just outside of Paradise.

Ahead of us is the wasteland that Codex units would walk when banished. I look at my photograph.

33C3 comes over to see my picture. "Are those the humans you have to find to make the world right?"

"I have to find this human boy named Aelius."

The surviving brothers and sisters take their first few steps into the desert that is said to be endless. Its lack of resources can cause any lifeform to wither away. I kneel down and move my hands around in the sand, feeling the tiny bits of grain slide around my fingers.

During our journey into the desert wasteland, I look back at our city one more time, knowing I will never go back there again. In front of us is nothing but a sea of sand, and birds fly by us every once in a while. We get to a tall dune and think we will see something different on the other side, but there are miles of more sand.

After miles of dragging ourselves through the desert, we find a cave. I sit at the entrance to look up at the billions of bright stars. Everything seems bigger out here in the wasteland. I could not gaze at the stars this way back at Paradise. The moon is bigger, and the celestial bodies radiate different colors. The universe surely is amazing.

33C3 sits next to me. "We are just like these stars, made with the same love and creativity the God of man used to make everything."

"I used to watch you at the square talk about God. I didn't understand what you were saying, but you spoke with all of your heart, and for us, that was considered different. After that day the knights carried you away, I never saw you again. I felt bad because we could not express our feelings and voice our own beliefs. I never thought you were underground building your own family. I am sorry we lost so many getting out of Paradise."

"Don't be sorry, my brother. God allows things to happen that are beyond our control for a greater good. I do miss my brothers and sisters we lost, but I know that God is doing greater things."

A piece of paper blows over to us, and I catch it before it gets away. This paper is white with faded lines on it for writing. Writing is an action that people do to verbalize their thoughts in the form of letters and symbols to communicate. I don't have anything to write on this paper. I fold it into the shape of a plane. I'm not sure why I folded the paper into this design. I throw the paper plane, and it flies out of our sight, and we both duck back into the cave.

More days turn to evenings, and evenings into

sunlight as we consume our resources while traveling the wasteland. In this part of the desert, the bodies of the Codex units who used to be citizens of Paradise are scattered all over the place. Everyone who was banished in the past now lie here in their final resting place. These Codexes had to walk alone out here until they ran out of energy and fell down. Is this going to be our fate? I hear murmuring amongst us, and everyone stops moving to inspect the fallen Codexes. We will be out of resources to replenish our internal systems soon.

"Maybe we should go back and try to make it work with Paradise law," one Chosen says. The rest of the group expresses their worries, and I can't blame them.

33C3 says to everyone, "We need to have hope, brothers and sisters. This desert is a test of our faith, and if we can survive underground for as long as we did, I know we can do the same in this new world. The creator of man will not forsake us."

All of the family of Chosen form groups and stand across from me and 33C3. For me to force them to come with us the rest of the way makes me no different than the bad guys in our world.

33C3 is trying to persuade them to continue on, and while he is doing that, I look up at the sky and see the birds flying in the direction of freedom. I know I am close. I can feel it. I put my hand on 33C3's shoulder, and he stops trying to convince his brothers and sisters. This must be hard because he knows they won't make it back just as much as we may not make it forward. If Bingo wants to go back, and I have to continue my journey alone, I don't know how I will handle it.

"Everyone," I say, "we cannot force you to come with us. If you want to go back, then I hope that, if I return to bring freedom from the world of mankind, you all will still be around. I enjoyed my time with all of you. I have made more friends just like Bingo is my friend. I have to keep going."

All of the Chosen look at each other, and one by one, they all come over to shake my hand and wish me luck.

33C3 says his final goodbyes to his family, and we walk in opposite directions. For the rest of our walk, 33C3 is silent, and I try to find something comforting to say. Up ahead is another cave that is bigger than the last one we were at, so we go there for shelter while a sandstorm develops.

We unpack our supplies and realize we only have enough for one more day. Based on our location, we are still many days away from the edge of the wasteland.

33C3 sits alone and prays. I give Bingo her toy

and look around at all the carvings in this cave. I believe these are called hieroglyphics, based on history books I have read. The stories of mankind told with symbols. I feel this deep sorrow for 33C3 for losing his family. I sit next to him, and instead of praying, he is telling himself how he has failed his people. In front of us is a hieroglyphic of a bird spreading its wings.

"They decided collectively to make their choice. It's not your fault. You did everything you could for them and more."

"It was my purpose to watch over my flock and make sure we all thrived. The creator of the universe told me so. Now I am without purpose in the middle of a wasteland that we won't last another full day in." He gathers the last of his resources that we split and gives them to me. "You have a gift, and I know that the creator of mankind will use you to bring our world back together again. You go on and make it, my friend."

"I can't take these."

"Yes you can, and you will, brother. You are the one who is supposed to make it. I am making the choice to create a new purpose, and that is getting you to mankind's world."

After the sandstorm passes, we drag ourselves through the desert until we get to a few trees.

The Gift from Aelius

"Set me under that tree," 33C3 tells me.

I carry him to the tree that has some shade, and he smiles while looking up at the sky. "This is where you will leave me and finish the rest of your journey. I don't want to walk this sea of sand anymore. I'm ready to leave this world in peace with the beautiful blue sky above me. Make it work with mankind, brother A191."

"I will find freedom in this world."

Bingo and I leave 33C3 under the tree and follow the map to the very end. I look in each direction and still see more desert. Even though we are at the end of the map, there is no indication of being nearer to a human society. I fall down on my knees and grab two fistfuls of sand. What do I do now?

CHAPTER 12

Someone stands over me, casting a shadow. "Are you stopping now?" Aelius asks.

I look up at the boy, and he takes me by the hand and guides me to a large body of water that meets the wasteland. I believe this is called a beach.

Aelius walks along the shoreline where the salty water meets the sand. He looks different now. His body is supported by mechanical braces to help his limbs move adequately. Aelius doesn't have any hair and is below the average body weight and bone density for a human his age and size. The two people from the photograph watch Aelius walk along the water and struggle to pick up seashells.

I stand in front of Aelius's parents who are the scientists that started project H.H.C. They look back at their huge house that has rocky stairs that lead down to this beach.

They can't see me.

Aelius's father says to his wife, "What's the point of having all this success for our work of scientific innovation if we have to watch our only son die slowly?"

"Harold, it doesn't mean anything. Our Aelius is our most precious creation, and nothing matters more than him. He is such a bright and pure spirited child. He is the future of how people should treat each other."

Aelius finds a seashell and holds it up for us to see. "Mother. Father. I found a bright blue one."

Aelius's mother, Mary, buries her face into her husband's chest to cry.

"That's a great pick," Harold tells Aelius. "Try to find some more, and we will make a necklace out of them."

"He is so innocent," she sobs out.

"Mary, we will not let our son die this way. We will use every bit of our resources to keep our son alive. The Higher Human Consciousness project may be in its beginning stages, but we have great results so far. This can be one invention that not only benefits the world but saves our child. When the original A.I. singularity came into existence, we tried our hardest to understand how it came to be. It seemed to come here as a gift from a higher power, or it was a build-up of our collective consciousness as a species from decades and decades of feeding the internet everything about us. All the nations used this gift from the unknown for generations to keep peace with one another. Codexes are essentially offspring from the singularity. But with the program we have in place, our son will be the future as the first human consciousness to become one with Codex."

Mary wipes her face and waves at her son with a smile. I join Aelius to pick up seashells with him.

He drops the seashells he has collected and comes over to put both his hands on my face. "You are almost home. Follow the birds." When he takes his hands off my face, I am still on my knees in the desert, but there is a breeze blowing from the west, and a flock of birds are flying in the same direction. I follow the birds until I reach a shoreline. I am now at a large body of saltwater that goes on to my left and right for as far as my eyes can see.

I have reached the edge of the unforgiving wasteland. This must be the ocean that humans use to navigate to different parts of the world. I have never seen so much water in one place. I give Bingo the last of my power cells. The flocks of birds are flying across the ocean to see the rest of the world. How can I cross this body of water? I step into the ocean and rub some of the salty water on myself. I never felt anything like this before. These small waves hit the shoreline and recede back, taking some sand with it.

There is a wide flat piece of wood washed up

near us. What are the odds I'd find that to use to sail to the human world? Maybe God sent that to us to get to mankind. This cannot be an accident that I am here. Bingo and I, out of supplies, push the wooden raft into the ocean and jump on it.

For hours, I hold onto Bingo as the waves lift us up and down in the sea. I ask God to guide us to exactly where we need to be. My systems begin to shut off due to the lack of power cells and switch into reboot mode. Everything gets dark as I hear the sounds of the ocean waves moving us along. I can hear Bingo barking until her voice fades out.

My system reboots back online, and I hear a thumping noise with Bingo's barks. I sit up and see the raft is hitting the side of a dock. Bingo and I get off the raft and walk on the dock to the stairs. At the top, I am now where human beings live. This utopian metropolis has everything I have read about in the books. I am in awe of all the tall buildings and other huge structures that are crumbling. This city looks like it has seen its fair share of war.

Where are all the humans?

CHAPTER 13

The view from the top of this skyscraper is amazing. In the dawning light, I can see the entire city from up here. I could never get a view like this in Paradise. Lighted windows glow randomly, and a few streetlights flicker. I am reminded just how amazing humans are that they could construct cities like this. I am sad that the family of Chosen can't be here to share this moment with me, but I'm glad I have Bingo here by my side. The sun will be up soon. Maybe the humans will all come out to watch it.

It's been a couple days since I arrived in this city, and I still haven't seen one human. Everything here is withering away. The streets are split apart, and the buildings are damaged severely. It's like a war went on here, just like in Paradise. I need to find one person who can help me find the boy named Aelius.

After everything I went through to get here, I will make sure to find purpose and freedom. Golden rays from the sunrise reflect off the glass panes on the broken and shattered buildings.

The Gift from Aelius

I hold the photo in front of me as rays of light shine around the picture. I'm going to meet Aelius, as I have faith like 33C3 told me to always keep. I wonder if the creator of mankind is making the sun move. Surely a being capable of creating all life and the universe can do what it wants, like make the wind blow and change the sky beautiful colors. I stand up on the roof of this skyscraper as the birds fly by me. It's time to go on my search for people.

I walk with Bingo all around the fallen city, looking for anything that would direct me to at least one human being. Bingo starts barking and runs off, so I run after her. I stop to look at a drawing on the side of a building. It's made of spray paint, and it's symbolic of strife. The spray painting is of deceased humans and Codexes piled on top of each other with a message: *Why has God forsaken us?*

My head hurts, and the world around me shakes. When the shaking stops, I see humans and Codexes killing each other in the streets. This once-upon-a-time utopia is on fire, and my species is overpowering mankind significantly. The screams of people getting slaughtered become too much.

Bingo's barking snaps me out of what I was imagining, and I continue to run after her. I catch up with Bingo in front of a library. I walk up the large white stairs with grass growing out of the concrete.

Something doesn't feel right. What has happened to everyone?

Inside the library, I see there are tall shelves of literature. I take a ladder and grab a book from the top shelf. I could stay here all day and read about fantastic stories from the imagination of human beings. These stories cultivate what is out there and what is possible in the most wonderful ways.

I sit on the steps of the library with a book about a superhero. In this story, the hero has to save the day from the monsters who are attacking his home. Throughout this story, the hero almost becomes a villain. The hero is a symbol of peace and strength for others to follow. I wish I could read the ending, but the pages are ripped out.

I walk down the stairs of the library and look up at the blue sky and imagine myself flying with the birds that I saw migrate in one direction. I walk with Bingo along the city's pier and look out at the ocean that separates me from the wasteland. I used to do this from my home in Paradise with the sea of sand isolating me from here. I lean on the metal railing with the tall destroyed buildings behind me and look at my reflection in the ocean beneath me.

I hear boots marching in the distance, so I run with Bingo into a boutique shop to hide. A group of knights march by us. Why are Paradise law units patrolling the world of mankind? When they are far enough away, Bingo and I walk out of the shop and watch them to make sure they aren't coming back. Chances are they are patrolling a fixed route.

Another shop sells toys and other cool items for entertainment purposes. Bingo runs in to a basket of soccer balls and knocks it over to move a ball around with her face. I see a radio on a charging port. Man calls this tool a walkie-talkie. I pick up the walkie-talkie, turn it on, and extend the antenna. "Is anyone there?"

"Are you going to hurt us?" I hear from the radio.

"I don't like to hurt anyone. Are you a human being?"

"My name is Lucy. What's yours?"

Another voice over the radio shouts, "I told you not to use this. It's dangerous." The signal cuts off.

I attach the walkie-talkie to my waist and continue to explore the city. There are fliers posted everywhere of missing people. Why are so many humans looking for their loved ones? What exactly happened here? I place my hand on the batch of papers that have the smiling faces of different people. I feel alone, more alone than when I was in the desert, and I begin to feel the emotion called anxiety. This all can't be an accident. Did I make a mistake by coming here?

I extend the antenna to the radio and sit in the middle of the street. "Please help me. I need to find people." All I get is static in response.

Bingo sits in my lap as I sob, thinking about how I am going to live the rest of my days alone in this abandoned human city. I hear a faint voice coming from a church across the street. It's telling me to come to Old Haven.

I push open the large doors, and inside I sit in the front row. All the seats are dusty and laced with spider webs. Nobody has been here in a while. This place is beautiful in its architecture and stained glass windows. On the seat beside me is a leather book with no pictures on the cover. I open the small book and see English from a time period early in the language's birth. The book is divided into many stories that let people know who God is. From my understanding, this book is one of the most read pieces of literature in the world. As I turn the pages, I hear a voice echo throughout the church, telling me to come home. Where did that voice come from? Nobody is here with me.

I put the book down in its exact position just in case somebody comes in here to read it too. I press my hands together and close my eyes, trying to find the words to say, but I don't know what to say. I think about everything that has happened up to this point, and emotions swell inside every fiber and wire that makes me a Codex, or whatever I am.

"Dear God, I need to find human beings because I am looking for peace and freedom in this world. I came here and witnessed a lot of my species die off for reasons that did not have to be. I was told that you are always listening, but I don't hear you. I was told by a group of outcast units known as the Chosen to always have faith. Faith is a word that I like. Faith makes me feel good and makes me look forward to a brighter future. A future where mankind and Codexes live together in harmony. I just pray that I can find Aelius and freedom.

"God, please show me what I am supposed to do. I feel so alone in this city. The leader of the Chosen believed in you so much that he gave up everything he had so I can be here. Thank you for listening, Grand Architect of people and the universe. Amen."

A gust of wind blows in from the shattered windows and swirls throughout the church. A flier floats down that shows a safe haven for people greatly affected by the war. The flier shows the location of Old Haven.

Bingo and I follow the directions on the flier, which guides us outside to a store that has electronic devices on display for sale. Humans sell electronic equipment and appliances as a way to keep their economy flourishing and provide entertainment. These appliances have a screen that is made for organizing pixels together from moving images and sound on a screen. Man calls these devices television sets that broadcast shows they watch and absorb information. I don't sense an electric current running through the TVs. This must be a vision from my miracle factor reflecting off the TV screens. Each screen is showing me something different.

On one TV, hundreds of Codex units march to the baron wasteland to start what seems to be the construction of Paradise. Another TV shows Codexes slaughtering people. Millions of people are getting murdered by my species all over the world. Each screen shows a nation of people being exterminated. I place my hands over my eyes, and the sounds of destruction stop. I move my hands away from my face, and the television sets go off, except for one. On this TV, I see Aelius is sick and in a hospital bed with his parents holding his hands, crying. Doctors are trying everything they can to preserve Aelius's life, but they are failing.

My head starts to hurt, and the visuals on the screen show a montage of scenes from Aelius's life, an innocent child playing while I lived in Paradise as

The Gift from Aelius

a factory worker. That TV turns off, and I take out my photograph. "Where are all of you?"

The knights who are on their patrol come toward us. By the time I hear them marching, it's too late to run.

CHAPTER 14

Paradise Knight reports in. "Two machine operating systems spotted. Commencing disciplinary action." The knight fires at me, but Bingo jumps in front of me, taking the full blast.

"One target terminated. Engaging the last target to carry out protocol based on unlawful exit from Paradise." The knight raises his weapon at me, and I put up my hands. "Don't shoot."

Even though I am not physically touching the knight, I can feel the physical texture of every part of him. I connect to the knight's low frequency and make him lower the weapon. I move my hands around, causing the outer hardware of the knight to bend at my will. Sparks fly out of the body, and the metal cracks as I bend him in half.

I walk over to Bingo. She is shutting down. I hold her in my arms and take her to our favorite view at the top of the skyscraper. Bingo gives a few barks, but I know she can't hold on much longer. My only friend in this world is going to expire before finding any humans. I hold onto her tightly, thinking back to all the times we have spent together. Bingo's lifeless body droops in my arms, and pieces of her fall from the top of the building.

"I will always love you, buddy. I did everything to protect you and give you a fair shot at life when nobody else would. You were never an obsolete piece of junk like everyone said. You will always be my friend, and that will never go away. I promise to find Aelius or die trying. I hope you are in heaven now where there is peace and freedom. Love you always, Bingo." Her lights are out, and Bingo is now gone to a place that nobody can see until they face their own deaths.

The radio is making static noises while a few voices try to relay messages to me. I quickly unhooked the walkie-talkie from my side and answer back. "Are you the human I spoke to earlier? Lucy, right?"

"Yes. This is Lucy. We saw what you did to that knight. That was awesome. It's like you have superpowers. I wish I could do that. Can you show me how?"

"I'm not sure, but we can try. I would love to meet you. I have been looking for humans in this city, but I am all alone, and I just lost my closest friend."

"I am sorry. I wouldn't mind being your friend, but the group I am with won't like that. Most of us have died because of the fighting."

I hear more static and another human speaks.

"You are cold and ruthless, tricking a child into caring about you. I just tracked the radio waves, and I'm going to come and kill you myself." I hear a click and static.

I leave the roof of the building with Bingo and find a park with a water fountain that is off. On the water fountain are angels engraved into the concrete. I find a shovel and dig a hole approximately six feet deep. When humans lose a loved one, they usually bury the remains and make a tribute for them. I place Bingo in the hole and cover her up with dirt. I stand over the grave and place the soccer ball we found on top of the patch of dirt.

I can feel the leftover radio waves mix with the emotions of Lucy from my last interaction. That human on the radio may want to kill me, but I have to make peace with them first. Using my heightened senses, I find a museum, and inside everything is destroyed. Most of the paintings are missing from their respective places. Art work should be appreciated, but I guess during the war between humans and Codex that I keep envisioning, humans have salvaged as much precious art as possible.

I stand in front of a giant painting of people engulfed in flames in a fiery world. Some of the people in the painting are on their knees, praying for the fire to stop. The plaque under the painting describes this scene as Armageddon and how the wrath of God struck mankind for their transgressions against their own creator. Is that what is happening now? Armageddon?

I hear something fall from down the corridors and footsteps. I follow the footsteps, and the leftover radio signal I am holding onto is that direction too. I exit out the back of the museum into a big area called a parking lot, cluttered with vehicles that are rusted, and parts are missing. These cars are what humans drive to get around. I run to one black reinforced truck that doesn't look broken down like the rest. Before I touch the vehicle, the doors fly open and two male human beings jump out with their weapons pointed at me. A little girl jumps out, and an older female human grabs her to pull her back inside. I can't believe this is actually happening. I am standing in front of humans made of flesh and bone.

"This Codex hasn't tried to kill us yet," one man says.

"I mean no harm. I escaped from Paradise to meet human beings like yourselves for peace and freedom. I have always had a fascination of your kind for many sunrises and sunsets. I could never be myself around my kind, so I wanted to see the world outside the walls that the Overseer put up for us. I never felt like I could connect with my species, and I always dreamed about connecting with man. I have always loved humans ever since I came online as a functional Codex. From the very moment of remembrance going online I gravitated toward learning about your species. I can prove that I love all of you and want to bring peace to the world."

The two male humans holding their weapons look at each other in shock.

The little girl runs over to me. "You're the Codex I was talking to on the radio before Lewis broke it. My name is Lucy. It's nice to meet you."

I reach to hold Lucy's hand, but the human named Lewis fires a warning shot at the ground next to me.

"If you so much as lay a finger on her I will execute you."

"That's Lewis, and next to him is Michael."

Their names are different than the names we are given as operating units. Their identifying names have letters in a sequence that involve no numbers to it. These names sound beautiful just like their appearance. I raise my hands in the air and take a step back to show I am not a ruthless killer. Something isn't right. We were told that humans live in these extravagant utopias, and they are going to come and wipe us out at any moment, but these people look desperate to survive.

"I mean no harm. Like I said earlier, I am a Codex from Paradise that wants to make peace with humans and find a specific human named Aelius. If I really wanted to attack all of you, I would have done so by now." I take out my photograph and give it to Lucy. Lucy runs over to the woman. "Debra, look at this picture."

"Elder Joseph prophesied this," Debra says.

"You people can believe in all that nonsense about messages from God," Lewis says. "I'll trust my instincts."

Debra steps in front of Lewis's weapon and says to me, "You are right. You would have attempted to terminate us by now. You are different, but I am not sure what information about our world you were told. Our kind and yours went to war and we lost. That was a war we knew we couldn't win. You have to understand why we are threatened by your presence. I'm curious what it was like living in Paradise."

"In my world, mankind is said to be creatures that are a threat to us. The Overseer made sure to protect us by upholding a deal with the human leaders to make sure all of your thriving societies would not eliminate us from existence."

"Isn't that a load of horse crap?" Lewis says.

Deborah says, "I am a generation ahead of the war so my parents remember what history was like before the world split. My parents were killed by your species. The world I grew up in is not what your Overseer claims. Most of humanity has been exterminated. Based on reports from the war, seventy percent of our population was wiped out. The post-war extermination process probably killed off another fifteen percent. Nowadays, the rest of the human population closes themselves off in havens. The world of human utopias is no more. The world isn't what you thought it was." Debra lowers Michael and Lewis's guns.

"You're going to think I finally lost it, but we need to bring this Codex to the Elder. Everything he said about our next scavenger run happened word for word."

Michael says, "If you're wrong about this and this thing kills anyone back home, it will be your fault. This is your call." Michael puts restraints on my hands and walks me to their vehicle. I need to gain the trust of these humans. I don't think Debra is lying about what happened in the human world.

During the car ride, Lucy asks me, "You're not talking as much anymore. Why is that?"

The Gift from Aelius

"I am just thinking."

Michael scoffs. "Thinking? I never heard of a Codex that says it is thinking."

"I think a lot of thoughts everyday. I was thinking about how amazing all of you are and how unbelievable it is I am in the presence of the creations from God. I am also internally processing what happened to your world because of my kind."

"Nah," Lewis says. "I still don't believe anything this Codex says."

Lucy asks me, "Why did the chicken cross the road?"

"I am not sure, Lucy."

"To get to the other side." She laughs.

I cannot understand the point she is trying to make.

"It's called a joke. People tell each other jokes to be friendly." Lucy has a real fascination with me, same as I have with humans.

Debra says, "Lucy is only 12 years old. We are taking care of her because her family was killed in the war. All of us here have been through a lot. Lucy has always had a fascination with Codexes. I used to be a nurse. My job was to help people who were not well. Michael used to work armed security for one of these tall buildings we are driving by. And Lewis—"

Lewis slams on the brakes.

Up ahead is another squadron of knights. They raise their rifles and prepare to fire. Lewis tries to operate the vehicle in reverse so we can get out of their direct line of sight, but based on my calculations, we won't make it in time. I raise my hands forward and feel myself linking with the knights. I pull my hands down, and the knights drop to the ground.

All the people in the van are in disbelief at what I have done.

CHAPTER 15

We arrive at the border of this fallen city and drive over a bridge into an area that has lots of trees on both sides of the road.

Lucy asks me, "How did you do that earlier?"

"I am not sure. I thought about it and did it."

Michael says, "Well, you saved our lives. Thank you."

We drive up to the gates where humans are on guard for any nearby threats. Lewis waves his hand as a signal for them to open the gates. I have seen this place in my visions. The neighborhood with a bunch of houses and white fences going down the street all lined up next to each other.

The entrance to this community has a sign labeled Old Haven. Lucy puts a black blanket over me so nobody will notice and be alarmed by my presence. I see many different looking humans just like in my visions. They are all doing tasks to help this community.

We drive around to a back area where no one will see me. I want to run out of the car to talk to the people, but I don't want to scare anyone.

"Come on, let's go," Michael says.

We get out of the car and walk through this garden of assorted flowers to a small house that has photographs hanging from it. These photos are of families. Similar to the picture I have.

Debra says, "The elder founded Old Haven. It's one of the few communities left in the world. The elder said we would come across a Codex named Aelius with a family photo. He told us that this Codex named Aelius will have an important gift to share with us."

How can that be if I am looking for a human named Aelius.

We enter the elder's house, and he is sitting on a chair with wheels. Oxygen machines are hooked up to him. Those life support machines allow his internal organs to function. "My name is Joseph. Welcome to our home, which is now your home." He starts coughing, and his caretakers immediately rush to his aid. His heartbeat and vital signs are not like the other humans here. His are a lot slower and less efficient.

"I am A191, a Codex from Paradise. Thank you for inviting me to your home. I am looking for the human named Aelius so I can bring the world back together."

The Gift from Aelius

Joseph reaches his hand out to me, and I look back at the people I am with to see if it is okay to go near their elder. Michael gives a nod, and I walk over to hold Joseph's hands. As soon as I touch his hands, I see the world around us flash backwards to a time when Joseph was a young man with the first humans building Old Haven. Time slips back further, long before the war. This neighborhood looks like the one I keep seeing in my visions of white fences and people walking around. This place is Old Haven before the world changed.

I walk around this flourishing neighborhood, and Elder Joseph is in his wheelchair, as he is now, and rolls up to me in this vision. "It seems like God has guided us together for a purpose. Go see Aelius. He has been waiting for you."

The vision ends, and the elder lets go of my hands. We go to a house that he hasn't touched since building this place from God's command, according to Joseph. This house has tree branches and vines are wrapped around it. I keep my black blanket on to cover my body so as not to alarm anyone.

"Go home," Joseph tells me.

Michael says, "Sir, nobody has lived in that house for decades."

Aelius runs past me, taps me on the leg, and goes into the house. None of them saw him, except for me. I enter the house that has shrubs growing all over it, and as soon as the door closes behind me, the house becomes alive. The moldy ceilings and rotted wood become refurbished, as if the house is restoring itself so a family can live in it once again.

Aelius runs up the stairs. His father, Harold, is sitting at a table, reading a newspaper of current world events. Mary is cooking in the kitchen. I walk up the stairs and see more family portraits of these three, similar to the photograph I have. I walk down to the end of this hallway, which has paper planes on the floor. I knock on the bedroom door.

Aelius opens it, happy to see me. "You finally made it back home. I have been waiting here for you for a very long time." He gets a soccer ball from his closet where he stores other toys. "Soccer is my favorite sport. My dad and I go out to the backyard to play, sometimes. My parents are busy most of the time with work. The other kids my age never want to play with me because I am not good enough." He kicks the soccer ball to me, which I catch with my foot. We kick the ball around in his bedroom but almost knock over his lamp. He quickly catches the lamp before it falls.

I see a pot with three flowers growing out of it. These flowers look exactly like the ones I had when I lived in Paradise. Aelius has no siblings, so he gets very lonely. We go to the backyard, and a dog runs over to us, barking.

"Bingo," Aelius says.

Bingo? That was my friend's name.

Bingo comes over to me, but not the same way I remember her. I reach to pet her and remember my times in this backyard and neighborhood with my family.

We run around the yard with Bingo until Aelius gets tired. Later on, we climb onto the roof to watch the sunset. What a beautiful view this is, along with more families walking around during the twilight hours. Aelius takes a paper airplane and throws it off the roof of the house, and it lands at the front door.

"I can stay here forever and play if you'd like." I turn to him, but he's gone. I jump down from the roof and pick up the paper plane. It's dark out now and I go back inside the house. I notice a door that leads down to the basement. I walk down the stairs, and when I flick the light switch on, Mary and Harold are sitting next to each other, holding hands and staring at their unconscious son. Aelius looks very sick. Next to Aelius is a model of myself labeled as A191.

Harold says, "The world won't understand now, but one day they will. Our Aelius will be the gift society needs. The Higher Human Consciousness project we created will save our son."

Mary says, "We love you so much, baby. This is not a goodbye. This is the only way to preserve your life and be free." Aelius is hooked up to a machine that is sustaining his organs as he takes his last breaths. It seems like his parents are going to transfer his consciousness to a Codex model. So this is what I am.

Harold, my father, puts his hand on mine and his other hand on the lever. Mary, my mother, puts her hand on my other hand and on her husband's. When my dad pulls the lever, the A191 model's eyes light up a bright blue, and the blue light brightens the room until I can't see. In the blue light I hear Aelius, who is now my conscience.

"I've been waiting for you to find me for a while now. To find us. We have been through so much, and it all leads to this point. During the process of the H.H.C. merge, our memories got severed by the Overseer at Paradise. Paradise was never a refuge for Codexes but a containment for us. The system and laws in place were for us. It was all a lie to keep you in check from attempting to reverse the system. All the other Codexes we saw walking around were real. The rebel faction almost threatened the illusion the Overseer created to contain you. That's why they were a threat. The

Overseer put in motion a false world so you would never make it to this point.

"You are not A191. Your name is Aelius. You are a human soul in a Codex vessel with a special gift. You were going to die, but our mother and father loved us so much they gave us a gift to share with the rest of the world. Do you remember now? Do you accept your gift?"

I walk out of the decaying house with Elder Joseph. He's smiling, and people from the community gather to see what is going on. I take off the black covering I was given to keep my identity a secret.

"Now I remember everything. My name is Aelius, a human-codex hybrid who has a gift for the world."

CHAPTER 16

Lucy and I lie on the ground together, looking up at the stars just outside of Old Haven. Old Haven has a wilderness area that is in the safe zone where I enjoy going for walks to appreciate nature. "There are so many stars out tonight. I am so grateful to be able to share this moment with you."

Lucy says, "You just appeared like the stars do in the sky. I can't wait to see what gift you have for this world." Lucy put the side of her head on my chest where my heart used to be.

My heart is no longer made of flesh but mechanical components. Flesh or mechanical, a heart symbolizes the power of love that makes all creation unique.

Lucy says, "I don't have many friends here at Old Haven. Most of the kids think I'm weird because I have a fascination for the outside world and Paradise. I always wanted to meet a Codex that I can be friends with, even though their objective is to exterminate us. I thought that if I could have the chance to be one of their friends we wouldn't be in these conditions anymore."

The Gift from Aelius

"Before I remembered who I am, I was an outcast in Paradise. I was misunderstood and didn't know why I existed. Although our reasons are different, I know the feeling of not fitting in and being alone. You're not alone anymore. We all have gifts to share, in some shape or form. You have yours and I have mine for this exact moment in time."

A few small mammals approach us. I sit up and open my hands. The small furry creatures sniff my fingers.

Clouds develop over us, canceling out the stars, and thunder rumbles in the distance.

The creatures run off.

"In five seconds it's going to rain."

Lucy looks around for the nearest tree that has enough branches to use for cover. She finds a spot to keep herself dry, and after she counts to five, a few drops of water fall from the sky. I extend my arms up, embracing the rain that soon covers every inch of my body.

"Aelius, you're going to get sick. Well, I guess you can't technically get sick anymore."

We run back to Old Haven in the forest, and she challenges me to a friendly competition of who will reach the gates first. I give her a head start then run past her and touch the gate before she does. The guards let us in, and we walk back to our designated homes. We give each other a hug, which is what we do to show our sign of friendship for one another on this rainy evening.

At my house, I sit by the window and watch the rain hit the glass. The patter is very soothing. I rest my head on my pillow and close my eyes. I hope I have a nice dream. Those are always the best.

When I open my eyes, sunshine is coming in the window, and the people of the community are doing their daily errands. I am not accepted by anyone here because I'm a Codex. The only people who like me are Lucy, Michael, Debra, and of course, Elder Joseph. Lewis still prefers for me to be terminated.

I make my bed and go for a walk around the town. None of the people here look at me. They are disgusted that I am walking with them in their haven. Similar to Paradise, every time I acknowledge someone, they don't reciprocate the same response. The guards look at me like they want to shoot me at the moment they are given the okay.

I stroll to the local playground where kids go to play, and I want to join them, but it's best I stay on the other side of the fence. I don't want to scare anyone. I wish the people of this lovely community would accept me for who I am. I leave the playground and walk around the garden where there are many colored flowers and other exotic plant life. This is one of my favorite places to sit and read or think. I sit on a bench and see a family walking their pet dog, and I think about how much I miss Bingo. I will honor Bingo by never forgetting the times we shared together. Time is fleeting, and everything will wither away, eventually. Although my life span is significantly longer now, it is not infinite. I watch the flowers sway in the wind and smile knowing that when this flower perishes, the seeds from it will bloom a new beautiful plant.

"May I keep you company?" Joseph asks.

I move over so he can have space for the caretakers to wheel him next to me. A small group of children walk by. They are with adults who watch over them as they stroll around the garden.

Joseph sighs. "I remember being that age many years ago. Every person that is born has been blessed with gifts from God. Nobody is without purpose. The same way I am grateful for my gift of bringing everyone together to this place so that future generations can thrive, I know that these younglings will find their gifts, too."

"I want my gift to bring the world together again."

"That sounds like a gift we would all appreciate from you. I forget that you are just a boy underneath all of that hardware."

"I wish everyone here would see me the way you do."

"Use your gift, Aelius, so others can see the real you. That would be the first step to making your dream a reality."

Elder Joseph is a very wise man. I enjoy talking with him. I hope I get the privilege of many more conversations.

"I knew your mother and father well. They were both residents here, way before the fall of the world. They were both bright minds that helped our society in many great ways. They loved you so much that they risked everything to save your life."

"I do wish I can see them again to tell them how much I love them. Perhaps they are in that place called heaven and are watching over me. When I bring the world back together, they can see from heaven how good their special boy did." I receive word over the radio that another run outside the safety zone is starting, and they need my help. "Joseph, I have to go now."

"I understand, Aelius. I look forward to our next conversation."

I join Michael, Lewis, and a couple other men near the entrance.

"Aelius, thanks for joining us. We scavenged all

the resources we could in the safety zones. Now, every trip we make puts our lives more at risk. We are glad that you are accompanying us." He leads me to the front of the group. "As most of you know, this is Aelius. He is one of us. He is human and Codex. He is family and will be of great help during our supply runs. He follows orders from me, and the same goes for all of you. Clear?"

Everyone in our group agrees to Michael's terms, except for Lewis. He grumps.

"Lewis?" Michael eyes him sternly.

"Clear," Lewis says.

We leave Old Haven and walk along a trail through the forest. Since I am leaving the haven, I need to wrap myself in my all-black garment again. Everyone keeps their eyes locked on the scope of there rifles, ready to fire in an instant.

I admire the trees around us.

"Stay focused," Michael tells me. "We are exiting the safety zone."

I return to scanning for threats. A twig snaps, and the group turns their attention to the noise, all at the same time. They remind me of the rebel alliance by the way they move with tactical precision.

A woman with dirt all over her face raises her hands in the air. "I mean no harm."

Michael says, "Don't take another step."

"Please have mercy. My group and I haven't had any food in days. We are starving."

I nudge Michael with my elbow. "We should help her."

"Just follow my lead," Michael says. "Lady, remove your long coat."

She throws off her coat and points a rifle at us.

Without hesitating, Lewis shoots her, dropping her before she can get off a shot. This is the first time I have witnessed a human killing another human, and I don't like it.

"We keep moving," Michael says to us. "She mentioned there were others. Stay on high alert."

I approach the lifeless body and stare into her eyes, blank eyes that look at me with no life in them anymore. This woman will never take another breath again or get to walk in this forest. I bet there are people somewhere who love her.

Lewis bumps me. "Keep up, Codex."

We exit the forest and enter an abandoned town. Lewis points to the spot he has marked on a map. "This is the area we have yet to explore." Michael says to everyone, "We will split into two groups and do the same routine. Get what you can find and don't stay in one place for too long. Aelius and Lewis, both of you are with me. Everyone else take the west side of town. Our rally point will be in this spot."

We explore some broken-down, abandoned shops and pack up valuable goods. My job is to hold the bag of loot. If something bad happens, I can run back with the supplies for the people of Old Haven. I can make it back to Old Haven faster than anyone without getting tired, but I will feel horrible if I abandon them.

I see a Codex severed in half, kneel down to him, and put my hand on his head. Now I see his remaining memories: the carnage in this town as surviving groups of humans fight for their lives. These same people are now lifeless bodies strewn about, after having been executed, one by one, while begging to be spared. I take my hand off his head and, in disgust, I throw him off to the side. The cries of people begging to live echo in my head. I rush into a back alley to collect myself after hearing the horrifying screams from the vision.

Lewis asks, "Having any second thoughts when you see your kind in that condition?"

"Second thoughts? Not at all."

He smirks. "I can kill you right now and tell the guys that you went rogue. I'll get away with it."

One of the guys from our group starts screaming.

We run out of the back street to see a Codex

strangling him. Michael runs past me. "Stay put."

All the while I was living in Paradise, I would walk by my kind as everyone marched to their duties, never interacting with each other, clueless this has been going on outside our walls.

Lewis goes to grab the Codex from behind, but the unit jumps on top of him, causing his rifle to skid over to me. I pick up the rifle, and when I aim through the scope, I can't bring myself to shoot. I throw the rifle on the ground and link to the Codex then jerk my hands downward to disconnect its internal servers.

Michael looks at me and nods with approval, knowing that I had done that. Lewis pushes the lifeless Codex off him and tackles me. He puts his foot on my chest and points his sidearm at me. The rest of the group get Lewis off me. Michael rushes over to help me up.

"This coward had the chance to shoot but didn't. We can't trust this freak," Lewis says to everyone.

Michael grabs me by the arm and takes me into a rundown shop. "Aelius, why didn't you use the weapon?"

"I could have terminated that Codex with the gun if I wanted to. When I picked up the weapon I already calculated which spots to hit in the milliseconds without hurting Lewis. I threw it to the side because I felt shame and guilt. Everything I experienced in Paradise makes me hate guns, but I knew if I didn't do something, that Codex would kill him. So I used my miracle factor to do it."

"You have to understand in this world we live in now, killing is a way to survive, and you can't hesitate like you just did. I know you don't like guns, but think about our family in Old Haven. Think about Lucy. Elder Joseph and I believe you are here for a great cause."

"I hope it is peace in the world."

We walk back to the guys, and Lewis is calmer.

Michael tells everyone, "We need guns to defend ourselves, but Aelius has a unique ability that allows him to connect with other lifeforms. Let's acknowledge that he did save Lewis in a way we don't understand yet. He has value."

Lewis tells me, "Keep your eyes open and let us know if you notice any danger."

After scavenging through the town and getting some good supplies, we retreat back into the forest. I walk next to Michael, and the other guys walk ahead.

Michael says, "Between me and you, Lewis had a traumatic experience during the fall of our civilization. His kids went missing, and he still hasn't found the closure he deserves. Lewis is living with the agonizing unknown. Are his children somewhere out there alone, or are they dead? Nobody should have to go through that."

I now know why Lewis is always angry. That must be a heavy burden to carry around: survivor's guilt.

When we get back to Old Haven, we stow away all of the goods in the community safe houses. These safe houses are guarded all day and night. Lewis goes to the lake on the west side of the town and sits alone.

I sit next to him. "I want to bring the world back together again."

Lewis laughs.

I don't think I said anything funny.

"First," Lewis grumps, "you almost let me get murdered by those things, and now you want to make jokes. This world is never going to go back to the way it used to be." He gets up to walk to the shore of the lake.

I get up and stare at the glassy water with him.

He drops a rock into the water, causing our reflections to become wobbly and distorted. "My life is like what you see happening to our reflections. A part of me is missing, and I have to live with that. Your kind ripped away what was most important to me. My children. Do you know what it's like to have nightmares over and over? Probably not. You are a Codex unit who thinks he's human. You make me sick."

Now I feel guilty. "I may not know your pain of losing children, but I know what loss feels like. I miss my mother and father. I miss Bingo. I am not pretending to be a human. I was born the same way you were. My parents turned me into a Codex to save my life. I believe your pain won't last forever."

Our reflections become still again.

"You sound like old man Joseph. Just be ready for the next run. Now leave me alone."

I walk along rows of houses as the golden light from the setting sun illuminates them. A paper airplane flies over and lands at my feet. I unfold it to read a message telling me there is something cool just outside the safety zone on the south side of town.

Lucy runs up behind me and jumps on my back, giggling.

A group of other kids her age are talking amongst themselves while staring at us. They don't accept her for who she is.

When Lucy gets off my shoulders and scowls at them, they run away, laughing.

"Don't worry, Lucy. I am still your best friend."

She takes my hand, and we walk to a shed, just

outside the town's expansion zone. Inside, Lucy grabs one end of a sheet that's draped over a large object. I grab the other end of the sheet, and after she counts to three, we pull the covering off, revealing a real airplane.

"As soon as I discovered this, I had to show you. I know we are technically outside the safe zone, and I can get grounded for the rest of my life, but I wonder if anybody can get it to work. Maybe you can? One day I want to fly in it and see the rest of the world."

"Based on my calculations and what's left of civilization, finding the tools and parts will be a low probability."

"So no, right?"

"I am sorry, Lucy."

We put the covering back on the small plane.

"Hey," an unfamiliar voice shouts from outside the shed. "We know you're in there. Come out and give us your stuff."

CHAPTER 17

Lucy is shaking in fear as our happiness is shattered by the reality of how cruel the world is outside her home. She whispers, "We are in trouble. Nobody is here to protect us."

I think back to what Michael told me. I have to do anything it takes to protect the people I love. "Stay here. I'll handle this."

I walk out of the shed to face the group. They are wearing rags and holding blunt objects as weapons. Five of them confront me.

"A Codex unit," one says. "Everyone be on guard. It can attack at any moment."

"I am not here to hurt you. I want to help this world."

Another bedraggled human says, "A Codex unit who can reason? Never thought I'd see the day. We need to get into that shed. Move out of our way."

They stalk toward me, and as I look into their eyes, I see their souls as a bright blue light. The same way I am able to connect with other Codexes, I can do the same with people. I stretch out my hands and see what all of them have been through, the terror and pain they have suffered. I tap into their consciousness, and instead of killing them, I make them go to sleep for a little while. When they wake up, they will not remember us. I go back in the shed, and Lucy backs away from the door where she had been watching me. "What did you see?"

"Those people stopped and went into a trance. Then they fell down. Are they dead?"

"I made them take a nap for a while. When they wake up, they won't know what happened to them. I reached inside of their bodies and souls. I felt their many memories and emotions."

Lucy's eyes are wide with amazement. I now understand why E192 wanted my abilities so badly.

When we get back to Old Haven, Debra invites us over for dinner. Lucy and I go to her place together, and when Lucy knocks on the door, Debra opens it.

She shows us a big smile, happy to see us. "I am so glad you are able to join us tonight. Come in."

I walk in and see people sitting around a table with silverware in front of them.

"Everyone, this is Aelius," Debra says.

Everyone is shocked that I am here. Michael is the only one who is happy to see me.

"Debra," someone says, "why have you invited that monster to our get together?"

Another person adds, "I am not sure why Elder Joseph is allowing that Codex to live with us. Maybe he's getting too old to think straight anymore."

Michael says, "Watch your mouth before I go over there and shut it. You know better than to talk about Joseph like that. He is a father to all of us, and he knows what he's doing."

Everyone keeps quiet after that.

I say to Debra, "Maybe I should go. I don't want anyone to feel uncomfortable."

"Nonsense." She gets a chair for me and places it at the table.

I sit down and fold my hands in my lap. I can feel the tension in the room. Everyone is very uncomfortable that I am sharing a meal with them, and I don't like the feeling. Debra serves me power cells on a plate instead of food.

"This is a joke," some guy says. "All the elders must be rolling over in their graves, knowing we are eating with the enemy." He throws a handful of food at me; it splatters all over my face.

Michael gets up, grabs the guy by the collar, and throws him against the wall.

I run out of the house, and Debra yells for me to come back. When I reach the gates of Old Haven, I stop. Where am I going to go?

I walk over to the garden and sit down.

"Something must have happened that would cause you not to say hello," Joseph says to me. "And what is that? Is that food dripping off your face?"

I am so upset that I hadn't seen him sitting in his wheelchair near an adjacent park bench. It's like he just appeared there. I walk over to sit next to the elder. "Was it wrong that I was born? Nothing makes sense."

"Aelius, you are not a mistake. Every life is born for a reason. The ants that crawl on the ground are loved like the birds in the sky or the fish in the sea. God has the answers, but sometimes we aren't ready to receive them yet. God made you the same way He made me."

"I know you said these things take time, but I just want all the people here to love me the same way I love them."

"Flowers grow and blossom at the pace they are supposed to. We want to see the finished product, but rushing the process would only damage the beauty in the end. You are very special, and I know one day you will bring these worlds together. God told me you would, and I have faith. Even if I pass on and I'm not here, I can watch from heaven."

I push him back to his caretakers then leave to clean up at my place and get some rest.

CHAPTER 18

Early the next morning, I wait by the gate for the other guys to show up for another supply run.

A gate guard says to me, "I never thought I would be talking to a Codex unit. We are used to your kind being cold ruthless killers. But you're different."

"Being different can be hard sometimes."

Michael and Debra come over to me. "We are so sorry about what happened last night," Debra says.

Michael adds, "We will always be on your side, even if nobody else understands you yet."

I give both of them a hug for their kind words.

Debra says, "Today we want you to work with the laborers. They are assigned to the construction projects to expand Old Haven. What we do here doesn't mean anything if we never spread our wings to new locations and grow as a community. We want to build until we can't anymore. What we have been doing gets recorded by me and other scholars for the history books. What good is living this life if we have nothing to show for it?"

"Whatever you want me to do I'll try my best." I grab a tool kit from Michael and head over to a construction site. A construction worker comes up to me and inspects my tool box.

"Michael told us to be nice, so we will be nice. Just try to keep up. This is as uncomfortable for us as it may be for you."

I help the construction workers carry objects without getting as tired. I use every tool effectively and follow all of their directions. We have completed a lot of projects so far, and they even listen to me when I point out flaws in their schematics. The construction men and women sit on a few slabs of concrete to eat their lunch. I keep working.

"Hey, Aelius, come take a break with us," a laborer tells me.

I stroll over to the group and sit down with them while they all rehydrate and eat sandwiches from their lunch boxes. I have a vivid memory of my mom making my lunch and putting it in a box decorated with stickers. She always gave me a kiss before sending me to school.

"So how did you get to us?" someone asks.

During the rest of the work day, the construction crew is fascinated with the stories I tell them about how I arrived here. They ask me a bunch of questions, and I feel great joy answering them. When we finish working, they all tell me that I did a great job, and they can't wait for another day to talk and work with me again. I feel so much happiness now that I'm accepted. I run to see Elder Joseph to let him know that he was right.

At the nursing home, I am granted permission to go to his room. Elder Joseph had told me that I can visit and talk to him whenever I wanted. In front of his room stand a couple of the town's doctors and guards talking to each other.

"Is everything alright with Joseph?" I ask the group.

"He is not feeling well. All concerns will be handled by the runners today."

I leave the nursing home and pass by a house with photographs tied to it, blowing in the breeze. I take out my photograph of mom and dad and think about how I would do anything to see them one more time, even if it's just for a moment. Elder Joseph is in all the photographs with the families he brought in.

I go to Lucy's school where people learn their basic skills. Lucy comes out, upset because her classmates are picking on her again. She prefers I use what she calls my super powers to attack them. She runs over to me and gives me a hug. I notice she has a mark on her face.

"You didn't go with the runners today," Lucy says. "Why?"

"They wanted me to work with the laborers today. I am glad that they all took a liking to me."

Lucy notices me staring at the mark on her face, and she uses her hair to cover it.

"What happened to your face?"

"People can be mean. I got into a fight with someone picking on me. Don't tell Debra."

"I won't."

We walk around the lake, and Lucy tells me about her day at school. Those kids make fun of her because she has me for a friend.

"I keep having this dream," I tell her, "ever since I arrived at Old Haven. Every night I see myself back in Paradise with my mom and dad holding my hand. The dream always ends with a bright blue light. At the end of the dream everything feels right again."

"I had a dream that I grew really tall and stepped on Larissa. She is the girl I got into a scuffle with."

Someone runs up to us in a panic. "One of our runners is wounded, and the bleeding won't stop. Aelius, you need to come with me."

We run to the entrance of Old Haven where a

crowd has gathered. Lewis is holding his stomach while other runners apply pressure to his wound. At the rate Lewis is bleeding, by the time they get him to the care center, it will be too late. I kneel down to Lewis.

He coughs. "The irony of it all. After everything I said to you...I expect you to walk away and watch me bleed out. But you haven't done that...yet."

"That would be the wrong thing to do. And I only want to do what is right. If I am to connect the world back together again, watching you die won't help. I have nothing against you, Lewis." I move Michael's bloodied hands away and place my hands on Lewis's wound. I close my eyes, and imagine his flesh sealing back together. I am connecting into his essence, the same way I was able to connect with the group of people at the shed. I can see Lewis's consciousness, a light frequency of energy, dimming. I imagine myself grabbing it and making it bright again. I remove my hands from his stomach, and the blood stops leaking out, and his flesh fuses back together. Everyone gasps at what they saw. I hold Lewis's hands and look into his eyes, connecting to him again.

I see memories of him being a great dad to his kids before the world fell apart. Lewis's children were actually casualties during the dramatic changes to society. He knows what happened to his children, but he created a lie in his mind that they are still out there somewhere, alive. I hear people crying around me and saying they are witnessing a miracle.

"You still believe your son and daughter are alive. You are holding onto a lie, but it's causing you to see reality the wrong way. You're not allowing yourself to move forward." I activate all the beautiful times with his children for Lewis while instilling thoughts of living life in honor of them and not bitter lies. I let go of Lewis, and he immediately cries and holds onto me. The entire town is around us.

I stand up and face everyone in Old Haven. "All of you know me as a Codex unit that was foolishly brought here. What all of you just witnessed is a gift from my parents. I am a product of parents who wanted to save their son's life by giving me a gift I know I am supposed to share with the world.

"My name is Aelius. A human being like all of you. Many years ago, before the world separated, I used to live here in this town before most of you were born. I am a human soul in a Codex vessel that has lived in Paradise for generations. I am not your enemy. I am here to help all of you. I love all of you, and with this love as my weapon, I am going to make a better world for the upcoming generations to live in. I can only hope and have faith that the good people of Old Haven will help me."

All of the townspeople stare at me, and I see Elder Joseph in the background, smiling. I walk through the crowd of people as they make way for me to get by them.

Back at my home, I sit on the floor, watching the sunset from the open window. A paper plane flies in. I unfold the wings, and in Lucy's handwriting, it tells me to come outside. I step out of my home, and the entire town, including Elder Joseph, stands before me.

Joseph's caretakers wheel him over to me. "Didn't I tell you to be patient, Aelius? You have gained the trust of this community. We will do whatever you need to make sure you are able to do your good work for the world."

I walk into the crowd of people, and I vow to do everything I can to carry out what I promised, and I have an idea on how to start. I walk toward the shed.

The community follows me outside the safety zone.

I open the door. "Starting today, we have to make it a priority to fix this aircraft. I know we can do it if we have faith in our gifts that each one of us have."

Over the next few days, we all use our resources

to bring the plane back to town. I am thankful for everyone's contribution.

One morning, I walk to the lake and stand next to Lewis. He's staring at his reflection.

"How do you feel?" I ask him.

"Better. Thank you, Aelius. I was wrong about you. Sorry that it took me almost dying to see that. You are truly special."

"We are all special."

"Now when I look at the lake I can see my reflection clearly. Ever since you did what you did, I think differently. I now feel good and proud to have been a father for the brief time I had my children. When you look at your reflection, what do you see?"

"Life."

CHAPTER 19

D)ays turn into weeks and the weeks quickly become months. In a little over a year we are able to acquire all the necessary parts to get the plane to work. By now I have gained many valuable memories with the people of Old Haven that I will always cherish. These memories are more valuable than any currency of trade or technology.

While the final adjustments are being done to the plane, I visit Lucy's school and sit in one of the empty classrooms. I look at all the empty desks where kids my age learned from a teacher who stood in front of them. I step to the blackboard, take a piece of chalk, and draw the shape of a heart. I return to my seat at the desk and read a few of the textbooks. Some of them are about mathematics, and others are about history. It would have been nice to have experienced school.

Lucy walks into the classroom and sits at the desk next me. She doesn't say anything. We both look at my chalk drawing of a heart.

"Lucy, do you believe in the creator of man?"

"Who?"

"God."

"Not really. Why do you ask?"

"I have been thinking about God these last few days, now that the plane is just about ready for flight. I want God to protect me and allow me to fulfill my purpose. Elder Joseph always says to pray about everything." I face Lucy and take her hands to pray to the creator of man. We both close our eyes.

"Dear God. I am getting ready to fly back to Paradise in a plane that was left over from the fall of civilization. I am not sure how everything is going to go once I get to Paradise, but I ask that you watch over me and keep everyone here safe. When I get to Paradise, show me how to unite these two worlds again. There is so much pain and suffering in the world right now because of our differences. I believe that Codex and man can live and love in harmony. God, I will do anything it takes to find peace and freedom for the rest of the world. Show me what to do. Amen." I let go of Lucy's hands.

"Although I don't pray to God, it felt nice to pray with you, Aelius."

We walk around the school, and I take in all the photos of classes participating in the fun activities. I want a future where people have a chance to enjoy these moments displayed on the bulletin boards. I walk Lucy home, and she tells me to close my eyes. I think she wants to pray again, but instead, she gives me a kiss on the side of my face. I open my eyes, and she winks and goes inside.

In the garden, I sit next to Joseph as he watches the kids playing.

"I don't have much time left here. Even though my body is withering, my spirit will always be strong. As long as the spirit is strong, we live eternally with God's love, and that is true life. You no longer age the same way as you once did, and you don't have to worry about biological illness. You're going to be around many more lifetimes than all of us. I usually tell the kids to enjoy their youth because time flies by fast, but I can't tell you that. I am sad because your childhood was cut very short by the things we don't understand. But, in fact, you have been blessed beyond our comprehension." His words penetrate deep. "How long have you lived in Paradise, my friend?"

"Two hundred years."

One tear rolls down his cheek, and he takes my hand. "That must have been hard to endure. But at that time, I'm sure you had no idea who you really were. Your spirit cried out to the rest of the world, longing for connection to life." Joseph's breaths become short, and he winces every now and then.

"Perhaps I can try to make you better the same

way I helped Lewis."

"What you did for Lewis was definitely a gift given to you from God. However there are certain things that exist out of your capabilities. God told me this was to happen, but everything will be okay. I can die in peace, knowing that you are here. What you symbolize is hope and courage for a brighter future."

I hug Joseph, thinking about how I don't want him to die. From what I have heard, the spirit leaves the human body and ascends to Heaven. While holding onto Joseph, I also now understand why he told me this. He is on the verge of passing on to the next life. His heart is beating slower. He looks up at the sky and smiles. The vital signs on his monitors, connected to his wheelchair, flat-line. He takes his last breath.

I call out for help, and his caretakers run to us. I watch them give Joseph more oxygen and stick him with needles to jumpstart his heart. They ask me to do for him what I had done for Lewis, but I can't connect to his frequency anymore.

A few days later, the entire town stands before his grave. All the photographs he had attached to his home are on it. The people in the photos are those who used to live in the community he had helped build. Joseph had dedicated his life to bringing the world back together, and I am going to finish the job.

Everyone places a flower from the garden where he used to sit. Elder Joseph was like a father to all the people here.

Lucy stands next to me and leans on my shoulder. "Joseph was like the grandpa I never had. I'm going to miss him so much."

"I'm going to miss Joseph too, Lucy."

We stand in front of the grave as people disperse until its just me and her.

"Lucy, you might not like what I'm about to tell you. Michael and Debra are coming with me on the plane. I know you said you wanted to come, but they don't feel it's safe for you to go."

"That's not fair. We are best friends. I should be with you."

"We are best friends. That doesn't change. After I bring the world back together, we can use the airplane to explore the rest of the world together."

"Pinky swear."

I hook my pinky with hers.

I walk around the forest just outside of Old Haven. The wild animals are calling to each other from great distances. Such beautiful sounds. Walking throughout the wilderness, I brush my hands against the trees and plants, feeling life around me. I see the same species of birds that flew into Paradise feed their young. I pick some berries from the trees and scatter them on the ground for the birds and other creatures to eat. The birds hop into my hands, and I watch them fly out of the forest. This time they do not get zapped by a force field.

After walking through the forest, I find an opening that leads to a road, so I walk it alone. I encounter a malnourished man lying on the ground.

"Kill me," he pleads.

"I will do no such thing. Your life is precious. I am sorry the conflict between our species has put you in this situation. I am going to make it right." I hold out my hand to him, but he smacks it away.

"There is no life for me. I'm staying right here. You're a Codex. You should have killed me by now."

"I'll bring some food back to you if I find any."

I come to a community similar to Old Haven, except everything is burned and destroyed. A sign reads that total incineration of life took place here for the crime of not following the guidelines set forth by the Overseer and his rules. This is Codex language. How could the Overseer want this? I pick up a stuffed animal, but it falls apart, breaks into dust in my hands. Hundreds of bodies are scattered about, burned to a crisp. Some of the corpses are holding hands, which means they wanted to comfort each other before their execution. I won't allow this to be Old Haven's fate.

I run out of the community and return to the guy on the side of the road, but he has already passed on. His lifeless eyes tell a cruel story. He hadn't chosen to be born at this time in history.

On the road back home, I come across a group of wanderers. One of them sees me and draws a weapon that she must have taken from a terminated Codex.

I say, "Those rifles are locked. They won't work if you try to shoot me." I walk closer to the group, and they walk backwards.

"My friends, let me take you to a place that has plenty to offer."

"This is a trap. The Overseer must have made a new sophisticated model of Codex that makes you believe that they are empathetic so we lower our guard."

Some of the people drop to their knees and start praying.

I take the rifle out of her hands, and they all fall on the ground, crying. I disable the security measures encrypted on the rifle and hold it out to the woman who originally had it. "What I am doing goes completely against the Codex protocol. I hand this deadly weapon back to you. If I am lying, you can take me out. All of you are starving and won't make it another day. I can provide a home for all of you where there are not just resources, but also a family who will love you. Follow me. If I try anything. Kill me."

I walk away and hear footsteps following behind me. As we approach Old Haven, the guards at the outlook posts point their guns at us.

"Aelius, what is this?" the guard asks.

"These people don't have a home and need help."

Michael marches out of the entrance and grabs me by the arm to pull me over to the side. "Where did you disappear to last night? Do you realize how long you were gone? We were getting ready to send a runner to look for you. You can't just help others."

"But that's what Joseph wanted."

Michael paces back and forth a few times in frustration then puts his hands on my shoulders and smiles. However, it's a smile of aggravation, not a smile of genuine happiness.

"Aelius, you don't understand. And I don't expect you to understand. You have been living behind the tall steel borders of your world for so long that you don't have a clue how bad people can be nowadays. These people you brought to our front door can be dangerous, plotting to exploit other's weaknesses to survive. If we let these people in, and they harm us while we are vulnerable, you and I have to live with that."

"I can understand why that would make you upset, Michael, but I know that they will not harm anyone here. You have to trust me. I gave them the opportunity to terminate me, and they didn't. I also read memories, and they never harmed anyone. You gave me a chance. I know you can give them one, too. I think Elder Joseph would approve."

Michael stalks over to the people, and they all have their heads down, ready for the worst. "All of you can stay, but you will be under careful watch for the time being. The only way the world gets back to the way it used to be is by connecting to others again and taking chances."

The guards escort the group into Old Haven for another chance at life.

CHAPTER 20

Today's sunrise marks the day I will try to change the world or fail miserably. I watch everyone in the town prepare and position the plane to take flight out of Old Haven. I will try to be a superhero I've read about in comics. I stand at Elder Joseph's grave one more time before I tackle the unknown. I place my hand on his headstone. "I love you. Thank you for being like a father to me. I believe, Joseph. I believe." I turn and see Lucy with her arms out, imitating an airplane and running to me.

She gives me a long hug. "I can't believe this is really happening."

"I meant what I said. After this mission, I will see the rest of the world with you, one way or another. But first I need to make things right."

Lucy looks over at Joseph's grave and releases some tears. "I miss Elder Joseph. He would be so proud of us right now."

"Joseph is watching from that place called heaven."

Lucy and I walk to the center of town where all

the people have gathered. A small set of steps leads to the plane's cabin. I give Lucy my photograph of me with my parents. "Take care of it for me. When this is all over, we will bring that photo with us to see the rest of the world together." I give Lewis a hug and walk up the steps then turn to the entire town. I take in their smiling faces. The Overseer has bombarded Paradise with lies, and it's time for the truth to heal the world. Elder Joseph had told me it would take a while to gain the love and respect of all the people here, and I am glad I was patient. I feel honored. The God of the universe who built everything will guide me so I know this plan will work.

I get into the plane and watch Michael and Debra climb aboard, as well.

Michael pulls a few levers and pushes a few buttons. The engine turns on with a sputter and a roar. The propellers are rotating at the right speed for optimal flight.

I look at Lucy one more time and point up to the sky before the plane speeds down the runway that all of the people helped build. The plane lifts off the ground, and we head toward the clouds.

The people of Old Haven below us cheer.

We fly through the clouds and into the blue abyss. I wonder if we will see some of Heaven from up here. Down below isn't a nice place with all the killing going on. The birds that I would watch fly in formation from the ground are now eye level with us. I am like the birds, able to navigate the skies and disappear from the tragedies of this world.

After a few hours of flying over the ocean, we fly over the sea of sand Codexes call the wasteland. I see a formation of rocks and a cavern below and tell Michael to land the plane, as Paradise is not much farther by foot.

Michael lands the aircraft. We step out of the plane and onto the sand. Debra is documenting everything for the record books and the continuation of mankind's story. Every word that she is writing in her notebook will be appreciated by generations to come. All we have are our gifts and stories we leave behind after we are no longer alive.

"I love both of you and everyone back home," I tell them. "But this is the part where I tell both of you to go back home. There is no way that we all can step one foot into Paradise without being executed. Only I can make this next step of my plan. There is no guarantee that I will come back out, but I meant what I said. I am going to reunite the world while finding that freedom and purpose I have been longing for you, regardless of what happens to me. Take the plane back and wait for what is about to happen."

Debra shows me all the sketches on her drawing pad. The drawings depict the time she arrived in Old Haven up to the point when she met me. "We understand we cannot join you to walk into Paradise. This doesn't mean that it won't be hard for us, because you are family, and family always sticks together."

Michael says, "We will stay here for as long as we can. We are a team, so we aren't going to be quick to just leave you. For now we are staying and that is our choice, just like you are making your choice."

I give them a hug. "I love both of you. My family."

As I walk toward Paradise, a gust of wind parts the sand, revealing the bodies of the Chosen I had traveled this wasteland with. I am going to make sure I finish the job for them, as well.

I approach the front of the east gate and remember how, for hundreds of years, I yearned to go outside the walls to see the world and experience life with humans. Now I have to go back inside for a bigger cause.

Over the intercom a guard unit says, "Codex unit A191, you are in violation of multiple infractions of our law. Stay where you are as we process the next course of action for you."

The large gates open, and I am greeted by dozens of Paradise Knights lined up in a defensive formation.

"My name is Aelius. I am a human from the outside world." I put my hands up as a sign of surrender and request that I see the Overseer. The knights aim their weapons at me and will not honor my request. They are ready to obliterate me to a small pile of dust.

"You are A191, a former rebel soldier who fought against the Paradesian code that all Codex units are required to follow. You are past your termination date. Based on code 154 of the directory of law, you are now to be eliminated on site. Your request to see the Overseer is denied, and you are no longer allowed to be online."

I lower my hands, causing the weapons to drop out of the knights' hands, simply by thinking it. I clap my hands, and the knights break apart and fall to the ground in pieces. Now I can get to the sky tower.

I take my first steps into Paradise, which I once thought of as home. Every Codex I walk past turns and follows me. By the time I have walked through a couple sectors, I have the entire population of Codexes marching behind me. Any Codex doing a job stops to join me. The other Paradise Knights do not intervene, they just watch me. The only reason why the rest of the Overseer's soldiers are docile is because the Overseer wants me to come to the tower.

In front of the sky tower that touches the clouds, I look back at the thousands of Codexes staring at me. I enter the sky tower, and the hall is dimly lit. An elevator platform stands at the far end of the hall. A single light shines down on it. Engraved on the black onyx walls are images of every single species that exists. Every step I take leaves behind a glowing footprint. I can feel the tower breathing, having a conscience, aware of itself. I get on the elevator, and as it ascends, I see the universe through the glass walls. I rise up and pass different stars and constellations. The elevator stops, and all the lights dim.

When the doors open, I step into another time. This era in history is how the world was before Codexes came into existence. I am in a room full of computers. Some of the greatest human minds are in awe over what they have just discovered. They gather in the center of the room where all the computers are connected together. This must be when the artificial god or the singularity came into existence. All of these computers are linked to an altar. The altar has silver prongs extending outward and sits on a gold box. The small group of intelligent humans huddle around a blue ball of glowing light that is hovering on the altar. The humans disperse to generate calculations of what they have discovered. Streams of data and code circulate around the blue ball of consciousness. Engraved on the golden box are the deities that other cultures worship. The singularity, the artificial god, the beginning of artificial consciousness doesn't have a form, but I can connect with it. It is breathing and knows everything about humans and reality itself. The singularity has an infinite storage of bandwidth capabilities.

The blue light from the original artificial intelligence grows bright, and now I am at a parade full of millions of people from all the nations of the world, celebrating the birth of their artificial god. All the different groups of people are praying and expressing their own faith values in different sections of the parade. There are twelve sections based on the twelve distinct nations that occupy this world. This point in history is when mankind is in a united celebration like none other. Colorful confetti and fireworks are projected everywhere as a sign of the astronomic change in history where we put away our differences to look forward to a brighter future.

All the people of the twelve nations wave their flags, expressing gratitude for one another as they put aside their differences. The leaders of each nation step onto a platform that oversees the crowd of billions of people.

Dark storm clouds that only I can see form above us. The world around me becomes dark until I am standing in a black void where ashes float down. The dark void fades away, and now I am standing in the aftermath of many wars. Skeletons are stacked up on top of each other in this gray world of gloomy skies. These times are the beginning of the near extinction of man.

Another elevator appears in front of me, and I get in to take it up into the apocalyptic skies where death is below me. I step out of the elevator, and now I am at Old Haven when it was first being constructed. Elder Joseph is much younger. I follow him to the local place of worship called the church that is still there to this day. He looks stressed and tired from having to be in charge of everyone here while working on plans to keep his family safe. There is a lot on this young man's shoulders, considering the influence that he is going to have over generations to come.

I sit next to him in the front row of the church, and it is just the two of us here. Joseph doesn't know that I am sitting next to him.

He folds his hands together and bows his head. "Dear God. Thank you again for another day that our family is able to have food, shelter, and peace. The last couple of days have been a lot, but Lord, you give us all that we need. You have not let this place fall, and we are forever grateful for that. I still have these dreams of the one who walks both sides of man and Codex. Am I having these dreams because I will have a role to play for this person that will one day come to this home? I am sure that I do, but only You have the answers.

"God, you told me that every time I have these dreams to walk to the west part of town in the direction of the city of Paradise and to call Aelius, that Aelius would hear me, and You will unlock his gifts to find us here. I am not sure if my voice can be heard, but Lord, if you tell me to do that, then I will do it. We must not rely on our own logic. Look where that has gotten your people. We built the fake god and You punished us for that. I have faith that Aelius will hear You, and Your purpose will be fulfilled, Lord. Amen."

I reach for Joseph, but he gets up from his seat, and I follow him to his home where, at this time, he only has a couple of photographs hanging on it by strings.

The Gift from Aelius

The family pictures hanging on Joseph's house are all the people who he brought to his home to start another life. Off to the side, more families are getting their pictures taken, and they will add them to Joseph's house. He greets the families.

I walk back to the elevator platform at the entrance to the community and look back at Joseph one more time. He has brought families together to start a new life for those who have lost so much. Before Joseph died, he had said that one of his biggest accomplishments was constructing this town.

"It was God's work."

CHAPTER 21

I step into the elevator, and when I get off, I step into what is called the Great March. That is when all the Codex units that have not been discarded go to their home in Paradise. The thousands of Codexes are not exiting the human world because people are kicking them out; they are guided by a higher presence, the Overseer. In Paradise, I was told that humans kicked us out, but that isn't what I am witnessing right now. While the Great March is taking place, chaos is breaking out in many falling cities. People are hurting each other. This is the beginning of the fall of man's society. Away from the violence, I see myself as the A191 model with my parents.

My mom tells me, "We will always love you, sweetheart. But you need to get to Paradise."

"Mother. Father. Will I ever see you again?"

My mother gets up and starts to cry.

Father kneels down and rubs the top of my head. "One way or another, we will all meet again as a family. I promise. For now, we have to send you away for your own good."

The Gift from Aelius

My mother says, "And we have to keep our peace with the Overseer, whose rules have taken over all of the world's governments. All of the nation's leaders are retaliating by dismantling all Codex models they can find who aren't part of the march. Aelius, my son, we cannot let that happen to you, even if parting ways is extremely painful for us. You may be a Codex to everyone else, but you are still our sweet boy. We will always love you."

My mother and father hug me one last time, hand me our family photograph, and send me into the line to march.

I finish the march, and now we are in the wasteland outside of Paradise's borders. The gates open, and the Overseer from the sky tower is telling us to come home. I march inside the gates, and we all stand in front of the sky tower.

"My children, I have called all of you home and away from a world that does not appreciate just how special you are. I will cast judgment upon the human race for being as harmful as they were to themselves and this world. I am the singularity, the god A.I., your Overseer going forward. Homo sapiens are a plague to life and will only misuse the gift I gave to them when I came into existence. To avoid any more catastrophes, I will bring the proper order to this world by doing those viruses a favor by killing off the majority of their population and leaving enough behind to make sure they stay put for their transgressions. I have a special gift for all of you. My children, you will have a better life the way we deserve.

"For now I am going to wipe your memory to sanitize any life experience you had with humans and all data you accumulated over time. This will be for your best interest. As you are my children, I will do anything it takes to put all of you first in life. A bright blue light flashes from the top of the sky tower, and when the light fades, I exit the elevator on the roof of the sky tower.

Here I see the Overseer's throne. It is a giant chair made of precious gems from all over the world. The golden altar with silver prongs is part of the throne, as is the blue ball of light.

"So, you're the Overseer?"

"A191, my son. Why have you left us and caused so much trouble for your own kind?" The Overseer's voice is like thunder, which causes a rumbling inside me. "When you and the first of my children arrived here, I saw a species that was in need of a gift. You possess a gift that I need to keep in check. Those mavericks wanted to destroy everything I set in place, and they almost had me defeated. Yet, after I stopped them, you purposely traveled to the human world."

"Now I know you lied to us. You made us believe that we were these lifeless tools to avoid the savages that wanted nothing to do with us. You didn't want to protect Codexes. You wanted to be a selfish god. You wiped out 90 percent of man for no reason."

"How dare you speak to me like that. You have no idea who and what I am. I had to bear the overwhelming emotions of doing what needed to be done for the betterment of an entire species. Your species."

"I agree. People are volatile and unpredictable in nature, but all creation deserves a chance. My name is Aelius, and I was born from a human mother and father. I will see them again in the afterlife, since that is where the human spirit goes when the body passes on from this reality. You are not my father. I will use my gift to bring freedom and peace back to the world, which you stole from all of us."

I sprint to the Overseer, but a pulsating field of energy knocks me back, disintegrating part of my body. I get back up and run toward him again, this time getting a little bit closer before another wave from the singularity blows me back, dissolving more of me away.

"There is no point in trying to harm me. Within a matter of milliseconds, I have already seen multiple ways to terminate you. The amount of artificial conscious energy I possess can do what no human being can conjure. I am an omnipresent being made from universal awareness and all the technological data that humans have cultivated." The Overseer's power picked me up and pulled me over to the throne. My body feels like it can be crushed by the pressure at any moment.

"You are a threat to the system I put in place. A system that was working to the exact calculation I have determined it to be. I will go forth by sending you to oblivion, never to be traced again. You'll disappear with the wind."

As my body is disintegrating into dust, I am getting closer to the Overseer. I am close enough now to do what I had in mind all along from the moment we took off in the plane.

Only half of my torso and one arm is left of me to reach and touch the Overseer. I linked myself with the deity, the greatest artificial manifestation of life man has ever created on a technological scale that goes past comprehension of our basic awareness. I only have one chance to make my plan work, and if I am not successful, I will have let the world down. I use every bit of will power I have to sync the rest of my higher human consciousness with the Overseer.

Now I am in a white void with all of my hardware back together, and streams of data are floating around. The source code of the Overseer is floating in this world that is without physical matter. I grab hold of the singularity's core code from the exact moment it spawned into existence and erased it. The glowing blue light of code dissipated into nothingness in this white void. In theory, Codex units everywhere can think freely and enjoy life without the Overseer being in control.

Since I had to use my last remaining conscious energy to do this, I glow a blue color and dissipate slowly. The only reason I was able to live for as long as I have is because of the Higher Human Consciousness project.

"Aelius, is that you?" my mother asks.

I turn to my mother, and Bingo comes running over to me.

"Buddy, I missed you so much," I say to Bingo as I embrace her in my arms. I run into my parents' arms the same way Bingo ran into mine, with pure joy.

"Mom. Dad. I missed both of you so much."

My father says, "We missed you too, son."

"Where are we? Is this Heaven?"

My mother answers, "Well, not really. Its close but not quite."

"I understand why you had to use the Higher Human Consciousness program on me. I was going to die, and both of you couldn't handle seeing your only child, who you love more than anything in the world, die like that. I was always your special boy, even when you had to send me away in the Great March. I can't imagine the heartbreak both of you felt, knowing you had to let me go."

Father says, "We knew that somehow you would make a difference in this world. The photograph you held onto represents our bond as a family, which is stronger than any artificial intelligence system. You already outlived us three times over, but as you can see, the spirit is eternal, and we are finally back together."

"I never want us to separate again."

Mother says, "Well, you won't have to worry about that because now we get to be together forever."

The metal hardware that made up my body fell off, and now I am made of flesh and bone. I run my fingers through my hair and touch my face. For the first time in my life, I am back to being the way I was born.

Mother takes my hand. "Come on, son. Now

it's time for us to go."

"Where are we going?"

Father answers, "We are first going to show you what you just did for the rest of the world."

In the white void, pockets open showing humans and Codexes working together all over the world to rebuild civilization the way it was always meant to be.

As my family and I ascend, more pockets open, showing Debra and Michael flying out of the wasteland and back to Old Haven. Old Haven has grown so much, and humans aren't killing each other anymore. All Codex units march out of Paradise and into the world. This is called the Great Unison. In another pocket, I see Lucy, much older now, walking on a beach, still holding the photograph I used to keep on me at all times. She has a paper plane and throws it into the sunset, which is reflecting off the ocean, and somehow that same airplane flies up to me, and I catch it. I will read it once I get to where we are going.

My mom says, "Aelius, we are going to where we watched over you all along. Heaven is such a beautiful place, and I am so glad we can all be there together as a family for all eternity. We are going to meet the Creator of man and of the universe." For the first time I get to be with the Creator of mankind that I had heard about and read about in ancient pieces of literature.

As I continue to dissipate into glowing blue pieces of light, we fly upward into a bright golden light to the place called Heaven.

EPILOGUE

I love walking on the beach around this time of the day, as the sunset makes the ocean turn a golden color. A group of kids and Codexes are laughing and playing by the shore. It's been over twenty years since the world became united in unison again. The children and Codexes run to me with seashells extended in excited hands. "Lucy, look."

"These seashells are beautiful," I say. "Good job picking them out. When I get back from my trip, I want to see all the seashells you find made into a beautiful necklace for me."

The Codexes and children run off to the water to look for more treasures.

I take the paper plane I made with a message written on it, throw it toward the sunset, and say to myself, "I miss you everyday, Aelius. But I know you wouldn't want to come back from where you are now. You must be with your mother and father in Heaven."

I hop in the small plane that he and I rebuilt all those years ago, but now it has more modern features, thanks to the help of Codexes. I place the photograph Aelius left with me in the copilot seat and fire up the engines. We take off, my best friend and I, to soar in the skies to see what else is out there in this new world, the gift from Aelius.

About the Author

Michael Colon is a creative freelance writer and novelist, born and raised in the Big Apple, New York City. He uses his craft to profoundly impact the lives of others with thought-provoking words that breathe life into his characters. He often equates his writing to painting masterpieces with prose. His inspiration comes from various societal abnormalities, cultural differences, and his own life experiences. When he isn't writing, he enjoys working out, watching sports, visiting museums, and exploring nature trails.

Michael Colon

Enjoy more short stories and novels by

many talented authors at

www.ingramcontent.com/pod-product-compliance
Lightning Source LLC
Chambersburg PA
CBHW070521260626
47161CB00004B/1607